Blood Creek

Fifteen years earlier five unruly sons of rich parents had committed a heinous crime against a young Ute woman, only to walk away unpunished.

But now a ruthless killer bent on revenge is stalking those boys, murdering their wives and destroying their lives piece by piece.

After manhunter Calin Travers is mysteriously attacked, then lured under false pretences to Sundown, Colorado, a town to which he swore he'd never return, he discovers himself face to face with old guilts and a vengeful killer who has marked him for death.

Blood Creek

Lance Howard

A Black Horse Western

ROBERT HALE · LONDON

© Howard Hopkins 2008
First published in Great Britain 2008

ISBN 978-0-7090-8454-9

Robert Hale Limited
Clerkenwell House
Clerkenwell Green
London EC1R 0HT

www.halebooks.com

Typeset by
Derek Doyle & Associates, Shaw Heath
Printed and bound in Great Britain by
Antony Rowe Limited, Wiltshire

For Tannenbaum

Please visit Lance Howard on the web at:
www.howardhopkins.com

CHAPTER ONE

There was going to be hell to pay.

Carla Foster felt it in her bones, even before she went to the window and saw the approaching rider.

He rode toward the cabin like a dirge, surrounded by an aura of shadow. A dark duster rippled under the midday breeze and the hazy sunlight that filtered through a gauze of gunmetal clouds shunned him. The brim of a low-slung felt hat obscured the rider's face.

That rider was one of her husband's loose ends, though she couldn't have told why she thought that. She just knew it to be true, the same way she knew death rode with that rider.

Jim Foster had done something, somewhere in his past. She wasn't aware of what this particular transgression might be, but it had come back to haunt him.

To make him pay.

Of her husband's past she knew precious little. But she had witnessed his brooding moods and fits of temper; they were the mark of a man consumed by remorse, guilt.

It was ironic she worried about such things now, wasn't it? She should have fretted over something like that before marrying the man after a mere two-week courtship. But how many men would have courted a woman with a past? How many men would have wanted a woman who'd strayed? How many men would have wed a woman who'd lain with too many men to count for a dollar a turn?

Perhaps he'd married her because of his own guilt, or perhaps out of pity. Perhaps a measure of each. At the time she had questioned neither his attention nor his proposal. Now it was too late to do so.

Their life wasn't a bad one, certainly better than the hell she had lived working in saloons across Colorado Territory. They got by. She'd learned new skills, ones that didn't involve opening her thighs to strangers, and he owned a small blacksmith business in town.

But they had never become as close as she felt a husband and wife should be. A distance always remained between them, something to do with the unspoken darkness he relived in nightmares and haunted moments. Over time, she had accepted his quirks, his ghosts; she no longer questioned him about it. She'd grown weary of him lying to her whenever she did bring it up.

Did he really love her? Had he learned to care about the woman he lay with each night but rarely touched over the past ten years of their union? She reckoned he did, and he treated her respectfully for the most part, provided whatever she required. He'd even blessed her with the one thing in her life that meant the most – their seven-year-old daughter, Clarissa.

A shiver traveled down her spine as her eyes focused again on the approaching rider. He had cut the distance between himself and the cabin by a hundred yards, but she could tell no more about him now than she had been able to a few moments before. He kept his head down, like a pallbearer.

She drew back from the window, praying to God the rider hadn't seen her. She noticed her hands starting to shake for no real reason other than the dark worry building in her mind. She twisted at the corners of her flowered powder-blue apron, fingers bleaching.

'Mommy?' a child's voice came from behind her.

She turned to see her daughter staring at her, puzzlement and a touch of concern on her delicate features.

Carla Foster had never been a beautiful woman, mostly just what folks called handsome. She had some bosom and ripeness of hip, but she reckoned she was little more than simply passable in looks. But Clarissa, Clarissa had been born beautiful and with each passing year grew even more so. That little girl was her angel and the Almighty had blessed that angel, and blessed Carla.

A surge of the dread told her that perhaps that

gift was about to be torn away.

'Mommy, what's wrong?' the little girl asked when Carla made no attempt to reply.

'Nothing . . .' she answered, too fast. 'Nothing, honey. Go back to your doll.'

A ragged doll dangled by an arm from the little girl's hand and Clarissa hugged it to her bosom, even at her young age plainly aware of the lie in her mother's voice.

The sound of hoofbeats reached her ears, slow, methodical, inexorable, and Carla couldn't suppress a start.

The rider was very close now, almost to the house.

Worry strengthened on her face and she saw it reflected in her little girl's eyes.

'Please, Clarissa, go to your room and don't make a sound.' Carla couldn't stop a measure of panic from leaking into her voice.

'What's wrong, Mommy?' The girl's own voice took on a note of fear.

'Hush, child. Just do as I tell you. It's just a stranger. Whatever he wants, I'll send him away. Your pa will be home soon, anyway.'

With that she turned from the girl to stare at the front door, her heart starting to bang against her ribs and a syrupy weakness trickling through her legs. Despite what she'd told her daughter, she knew she wouldn't be able to send this stranger away. She knew it and it scared the hell out of her.

Behind her the little girl backed up a few paces but didn't leave the parlor. Tiny lights of worry jiggered in her china-blue eyes.

The hoofbeats stopped.

Carla's heart jumped into her throat with the thud of the first bootfall on the old porch boards.

'He's not going to go away . . .' she whispered, lower lip quivering, fingers twisting harder at the fabric of her apron. 'He's not going to go away.'

A knock sounded on the door, not especially hard, but it might as well have been a death knell the way it made her shudder.

'You're scaring yourself for no reason,' she tried to assure her jangled nerves, but couldn't make herself believe it.

She made no move toward the door. She wasn't sure she could have taken a step forward had she tried.

Another knock. More insistent. He knew she was in here. He *knew* it and would never go away until she opened that door and invited death into the house.

'Please . . .' Her voice came weaker than she intended. 'Please, go away. There's nothing here for you . . .'

A laugh sounded from beyond the door, a dark sound, low, laced with the promise that yes, there was indeed something in this house he wanted and he would not depart until he got it.

Another knock. Harder. Like gunshots.

'Please, just go away!' she yelled suddenly, fear raising her voice to a shrill pitch.

'Open the door, ma'am . . .' a voice came from outside.

'Please, just leave us be . . .'

'Afraid I can't do that, ma'am. I got business . . .'

'My husband's in town. He'll be back soon. You can talk to him then.'

'I intend to, ma'am. But my first order of business is with you—'

A crash sounded and she nearly came out of her skin. The door flew inward, rebounded from the wall; the man stopped it with a flattened palm.

He took a step inward, his head lifting so she could see his dark eyes, his devil eyes. He had a young face, yet somehow old at the same time, weathered and brown, pure-blood Indian of some sort. Cruel. If she had been forced to pick a word to describe his features she would have used cruel. Something was missing from his eyes, something . . . *human*. He was driven by evil, this man, a force dark and sinister that was now focused on her.

'You aren't unattractive, but nothing like Crying Dove.' He came further inside, easing the door shut behind him. The door didn't latch, its mechanism broken by his kick, and fell open a crack. She glimpsed a Bowie knife strapped to his thigh as his duster parted, but no gun.

A small scream came from behind her and her head twisted. She saw terror on her daughter's face.

The stranger's gaze jumped to the girl and a peculiar expression washed over his dark face, not a smile exactly, not a frown, either. A certainty.

'Quiet, now, child,' the man said. 'You won't be forced to watch . . .'

12

Carla began backing toward her daughter, her gaze flicking to a shotgun on wall pegs above the fireplace mantel. Could she reach it in time?

She had to try. She made a move in that direction but he was suddenly beside her, grabbing her arm and twisting hard. She bleated in pain as he whirled her around. His free hand flashed up, fist taking her full across the face. Pain lanced through her teeth and her legs went out from under her. She collapsed, hitting the floorboards hard, breath knocked from her lungs, vision blurred.

The stranger stepped over her and reached beneath his duster into a hidden pocket. He drew out four railroad spikes and dropped them with a clank on to the floor.

The mist swept from Carla's vision as he again reached beneath his duster and withdrew pieces of rope, then dropped them beside the spikes.

'Please ... don't hurt us ...' she whispered, trying to move backward.

He stepped on her foot, stopping her, and she winced.

'I won't hurt the girl. I promise. Unfortunately, I can't promise you the same.'

A tear slipped down Carla's cheek. Her voice shook. 'I don't even know you. Why, why are you doing this?'

Darkness filtered across his face. For what felt like an eternity he remained silent, staring down at her. 'Because I have to. Because your husband forced me to the day he ...' He stopped, dark eyes suddenly shimmering with tears. 'They all have to pay for what they did . . .'

His hand went to his thigh and he withdrew the Bowie. Muted light arcing through the window glinted off the blade.

Jim Foster could not recollect how many times he had thought of telling Carla about his past, about that day at Blood Creek. About the day he'd irrevocably blackened his soul.

But how could he? How could a man tell his wife the things that ravaged his nightmares and soiled the very core of all he was?

How could he tell her how the terror on a young woman's face had burned into his memory?

That girl had teased them, led them to do it, he'd tried to assure himself, but he knew it was merely an excuse. They should have known when to stop. Rationalizing the act would do nothing to relieve the guilt that tortured him, at least in the long run. He had to tell Carla someday, had to trust she loved him enough to understand and forgive. Trust her to see why he'd been so cold to her, despite the fact she meant more to him than anything in the world. If he didn't tell her it would kill him, and worse it would destroy any chance at happiness they had left.

But he wouldn't tell her, not today. Because the moment he stepped through that door and saw her face, his resolve would falter and as on a hundred other days he would not go through with it. Because he was too ashamed, and it was too risky, the chance of losing her when she found out what he'd done.

And nothing in this world frightened Jim Foster more than losing that woman and their child.

He rode slowly towards the house, taking in a great drink of spring-freshened air and shaking with the memory of that day long past. What had become of that young Indian woman? He asked that question of himself daily. Had she gone back to her band with that brave who tried to stop them? Had she regained face amongst her people? Indians were peculiar in their ways, how they saw things. But, then, even many white men would have judged a woman soiled after such an act.

Questions. Too many questions with no answers. Only guilt. Remorse.

He gigged the horse into a faster gait, knowing he was stalling his arrival home as he had done countless times before. He was guilty; he would just have to live with it the rest of his days and that was that.

You might have stopped it if you had stood up with Travers . . .

Could he have stopped the others? While he doubted it, the question remained. They would have done to him what they did to Travers, but perhaps there would have been a chance. . . .

And what after that? Those boys were too powerful, their folks too rich. He would have been ostracized, the way Travers had been. He would have never had a moment's peace.

Foster uttered a strained laugh. Did he have peace now?

What about the others? Did they face the same ghosts as he every hour of every day and every night? Did they feel the same gut-wrenching shame? If only repentance were as easy as the pastor in town made it out to be.

But acts committed, whether in youth or manhood, came with cost and consequence so much easier to consider after the fact than before.

A strange feeling wandered through him as he reached his cabin. At first he wasn't certain what caused it. It dawned on him there was another horse there, tied to the hitchrail, a palomino he didn't recognize. Who could have come to the small ranch? No one ever visited and they had no real friends. By his own decree they remained much more isolated than Carla would have liked.

Yet the feeling, now distinguishing itself as dread, increased and sent a shiver down his back. He reined to a halt, sat studying the animal. Lips pursed, brow crinkled, making the map of lines across his face deepen, he wondered why he felt the way he did. He saw no tangible reason for it. It was simply a notion, one he could not deny.

He pushed up his battered hat, then rubbed at his stubbly chin. With a sigh, he tied to shake off the feeling, not entirely successfully. The fact remained someone had come to his cabin and that just didn't happen.

There's trouble . . . he thought, as he dismounted.

He rubbed at his lower back, muscles stiff and bones aching from blacksmithing for the better part of the day. He hitched his mount beside the other horse and made his way up the rickety steps to the porch. Pausing as he reached the door, he knew suddenly the sinking dread in his belly was justified.

The door was open a crack and the latch was splintered.

He swallowed, sure as a man gazing upon his own noose could be that any chance he might have had at redemption for his sins was now lost.

Jim Foster was a large man, and his trade made his arms and hands powerful, but suddenly he shook like a newborn calf. Someone was in that house, someone from the past. And once he stepped through that door there was no going back. Nothing would be the same. Ever. His ghosts had come to destroy him.

Nonsense, he told himself, trying to get a grip on his composure. His hand went to the Smith & Wesson holstered at his hip, gripped the handle so hard his knuckles went white.

With his left hand he gave the door a slight push. It creaked inward, wobbling on loose hinges.

The sight that greeted him instantly washed away any semblance of courage and resolve he might have gathered. His mouth fell open and a small sound escaped, one pregnant with terror.

'Jesus, Carla . . .' He blundered across the threshold, driven by the sight of his wife staked to the floor, heedless of all caution.

17

The sight lasted only a second because he glimpsed a knife hilt just before it slammed into his temple and blackness swallowed his senses.

Jim Foster didn't know how long he'd been out but when he regained consciousness a kerosene lantern burned on a small table and dusk had fallen. His skull throbbed and his vision refused to focus.

The memory crashed back in, the sight of his wife staked to the floor, and a rushing torrent of fear cleared his mind. 'You are awake, Jim Foster.'

'W-What?' he mumbled, head lifting, the effort making his senses swim and his head bang more intensely. He looked up, vision clearing. A dark figure stood above him.

'I was afraid I had killed you. That would not have fit into my plan.' The voice was low, damning.

Jim Foster's eyes narrowed as he tried to pierce the darkness beneath the figure's low-pulled hat, but he couldn't see the man's features, except for a square, solid chin. Strands of long hair straggled to the man's shoulders and his build under the duster was stocky.

'Who . . . who are you. . . ?' An ice-pick of pain stabbed his temples and he winced, tried to raise his hand to his head, but quickly discovered it wouldn't move. He looked at his hand, a puzzled expression crossing his features. Both wrists were tied to the leg of the sofa and ropes surrounded his body as he sat hunched on the floor, angled towards his wife and the figure that poised above him.

18

'Carla . . .' he whispered. 'Please, God, no . . .'

The figure stepped back, letting him see Carla where she lay in the middle of the parlor, legs and arms splayed, wrists and ankles each tied to a railroad spike driven into the floorboards. Her dress was shredded, barely covering her bruised and battered body. A bandanna was laced through her teeth and around her head. Her eyes glared wide with terror.

The dark figure uttered a humorless laugh. 'Do you remember, white man? Do you remember that day at Blood Creek and Crying Dove? Do you remember what you did – what you *all* did?'

'P-please, no, it wasn't Carla's fault . . .' The memory of that day crashed into his mind, blended with the horror of seeing his wife helpless before him. 'It was my fault. . . . Please . . . don't hurt her. I'm sorry . . . sorry for what we did . . .'

The figure scoffed, the sound ripe with condemnation. 'Fifteen years . . . and *now* you are sorry. Why? Because you have something to lose, as I did that day? Because you pray for the mercy you never showed Crying Dove?'

'We didn't mean—'

'The hell you didn't!' The figure's boot lashed out, taking Jim Foster across the chin, hard enough to break a tooth and bring a spurt of blood but not hard enough to send him back into unconsciousness.

Tears welled in his eyes, ran down his face. Not from pain but from the certain knowledge that what was going to happen to his wife would be unstoppable. He could do nothing but watch, and die inside each step of the way.

'Take me ... please.' His voice trembled. 'Take me. Let my family be.'

The figure's head turned, first looking at the battered woman staked to the floor, then moving on to the small figure of the little girl huddled in the corner, tied and blindfolded. The child sobbed, clung desperately to her ragged doll. The figure's head came back around, dark eyes focusing on Jim Foster.

'I will not harm your daughter.' The figure's hand went briefly inside his duster, withdrew. A Bowie knife glinted with captured kerosene light. 'But your wife ... I'm going to take her while you watch ...' He held the knife up, observing its contour, poising it so Jim could see it had been sharpened to a razor edge. 'Then I am going to peel her flesh back, inch by inch, while you listen to her screams, Jim Foster. And after her screams stop I'll hang her hide on the fence post out yonder to remind you of the day Crying Dove begged for mercy and you granted her none.'

Nausea flooded Jim's belly and he nearly came up with his stomach contents. Something in his mind began to unhinge, threatening to send him deep into a world of inescapable hell where guilt and regret were relived each second of each day of each year.

'No, please don't do this. I'll do anything, give

you anything. I'll admit what I did. I'll hang for it. Just don't hurt her . . .'

The man laughed again, the sound chilling, uncompromising.

'It is too late for that, Jim Foster. You will bear witness and remember this day forever in your nightmares, the way I remember Blood Creek in mine.'

'You're crazy, you sonofabitch!' Jim Foster's voice rose to a shrill pitch, one he barely recognized as his own. Images pried at his mind; guilt became overwhelming, terror all-consuming. 'I'll tell, I'll tell the marshal and hunt you down—'

The figure's head shook. 'No, you will not. Because if you tell I will do the same thing to your daughter as I do to your wife. Her life for your silence . . . that is a small price, is it not?'

The figure stepped closer to Carla's bound ankle and shucked off his duster. He tossed it aside and fondled the blade in his hand. He paused, looked back at Jim Foster, whose face was a mask of utter terror and pleading. Tears streamed and his head swung slowly in denial.

'You can't do this . . .' Jim whispered. 'Please, you can't do this.'

'I already have, on three other occasions. And I will again. You *all* have a debt to pay.'

For the first endless moments Jim pressed his eyes shut, refusing to watch as the figure clamped the knife between his teeth, unbuckled his trousers and climbed atop his wife. But Carla's mewing tore into his mind and into his soul. This was what Hell was like for sinners. This was what pure suffering and the agony of retribution was for the guilty.

'I'm sorry, Carla, so sorry . . .' he repeated in his mind a thousand times as the man forced himself upon her, but supplications did no good.

Then the sounds changed to screams and Jim's eyes came open to see the man, finished with defiling her, trousers buckled again, holding the blade at Clara's ankle, pressing it into her soft flesh until blood streamed. The man had pulled the bandanna from her mouth, leaving it bunched on the floor beside the bound woman.

Carla thrashed, yanking at her bonds until flesh tore from her wrists and ankles.

Jim Foster shrieked as the last of his sanity deserted him. In a fleeting shred of awareness he begged for God to spare his wife.

That prayer went unanswered.

CHAPTER TWO

'You Travers?' The voice came from behind him as he sat at the bar in the Bannerville saloon, nursing a beer.

The sun had set less than a half-hour ago and the glow from kerosene lights refracted within the haze of Durham smoke clouding the barroom. A dozen cowboys sat at tables, playing poker or pinching bardoves as they sauntered by.

Calin Travers had called it quits for the day, leaving his secretary to filter through over a half-dozen cases from which he had his choice for the following few weeks. He hoped they didn't all involve tracking wandering husbands. He'd been getting far too many of that type lately, but that was the price of fame, courtesy of some dime novelist looking to make a buck.

Calin Travers, thin of build but wiry of muscle, twisted on the bar stool to confront whoever stood behind him. He had not recognized the voice and the face that went with it didn't solve that problem.

Yet something about the fella put him on the immediate alert. The gent was square of build, hard of feature. His nose showed evidence of having been broken more than once; it sat at a peculiar mashed angle on his pockmarked face. Plenty of gristle bulged on his brow and a lack of sparkle in his dull brown eyes pegged him as a fighter and likely a hardcase. This was the type of man Calin usually wound up tracking down. The questions were: why was that situation now reversed and did this man pose a threat?

'Figure I asked you a question,' the man said when Calin simply surveyed him and remained silent. ' 'Xpect an answer or are you one of them dumb sonofabitches?'

Calin frowned, setting his beer mug on the bartop next to his hat. He brushed his brown hair from his forehead and slipped off the stool to stand uncomfortably close to the fellow. The hardcase stank like he'd spent three days holdin' on to the hind end of a cow and his gaze didn't waver. Nothing good was going to come of this meeting, Calin reckoned. He'd best prepare for it, now.

'I'm Travers. You got business with me?' He held his voice steady, refusing to show the slightest intimidation, despite an urge to take a couple steps away from the man and give himself some fighting-room if it came down to that.

The hardcase grinned. It wasn't a comforting expression. 'That's all I wanted to know—' The man suddenly threw a punch. It collided with Calin's jaw, rattling his teeth, snapping his head back and sending him spiraling around like a child's top.

Now *that* he hadn't prepared himself for. He hadn't expected the man to simply strike out without at least some type of preliminaries. Hell, hardcases usually liked to threaten or brag a bit before they pounded your bones into the sawdust.

Before Calin got a chance to recover, another blow pistoned straight at his nose. Having little desire to have his features end up resembling those of the hardcase, he tried to jerk his head sideways, but only partly succeeded.

The blow still rocked him, propelled him backwards straight over a table and to the floor. He landed hard, air exploding from his lungs, senses threatening to desert him.

'Goddammit!' he muttered, then spat a stream of blood into the old sawdust covering the saloon floor.

Around the room cowboys went quiet, watching in rapt fascination. One of the bargals working the room didn't freeze; she let out a shriek that could have woken the dead.

The bargirl, Millie, who had a thing for Calin, followed the shriek with a string of vulgar names and curses that likely had never even been heard on a cattle drive. Calin, through blurry vision, saw her grab a bottle and charge at the hardcase, swinging.

The hardcase spun, grabbed her arm in midair and whirled her around. He snatched the bottle from her hand, then hurled her over a table. She landed flat on her back, immediately struggled to get up, but failed, too stunned by the impact.

Calin jumped to his feet, angry at being sucker-punched and furious at seeing Millie manhandled. Blood streamed from his mouth and with the back of his hand he brushed it away.

'You sonofabitch . . .' he muttered as the hard-case whirled back towards him. 'Hittin' a woman . . .'

The hardcase laughed. Calin didn't consider that a particularly encouraging sign. This man, as he guessed from the mashed nose and gristly brow, was used to fighting and likely used to winning.

'Way I see it, gent, I hit *two* women . . .' The hard-case stepped forward, cocking an arm, preparing to launch a finishing blow.

Calin's green eyes narrowed. His gaze locked with the other man's.

The hardcase swung.

Calin doubled; the blow whisked over him. In nearly the same move, he bobbed back up, snapping a short uppercut. He was still a little shaky but the force of the blow cracking the hardcase's chin made a sound like two blocks colliding and stopped the man in mid-swing.

Calin might have been thin, wiry, but he'd spent the past ten years building his strength, vowing never to lose another fight.

The hardcase blinked, stared stupidly at nothing for a moment, then shook his head and let out something as close to a roar as Calin had ever heard come out of a human being.

Another bad sign. Calin had taken out men twice his size with that punch. This time it had only served to piss the fella off.

The hardcase bellowed and grabbed two handfuls of Calin's shirt. He hauled the manhunter straight off the floor, then flung him sideways.

'Jesus!' Calin muttered as he flew a good six feet and crashed into the floor in a cloud of sawdust and pain.

He rolled, cushioning the majority of the impact this time, but his left side hurt like a mule had kicked him. A memory flashed through his mind: fists pounding him, feet kicking him, his blood dripping into a sandy creek bank.

The memory was mercifully short-lived because the hardcase came lumbering toward Calin, who was struggling to push himself up on to hands and knees, and launched a kick that sent him flying over on to his back.

Calin groaned, nausea flooding his belly and welts of agony spiking through his ribs. He'd be lucky if none had been broken. If he survived this they sure as hell were going to ache for a week or two.

'Get up, girly,' the hardcase said, a lilt in his voice that showed he was damn well enjoying kicking the cow chips out of a man smaller than he.

Calin rolled on to his belly, dragged his arms to his shoulders and pressed his hands into the floor. He pushed, making it to his hands and knees this time, but only because the hardcase was too busy reveling in his domination over his opponent to bother kicking him again.

Calin's mind raced. No one else in the room made a move to help him and he reckoned he had only himself to blame for that. Everyone in this town knew his reputation for winning fights and were likely so goddamned spellbound by the sight of him getting shellacked they neglected to bother stepping in. Plus he reckoned they were too damned afraid of any man who could get the jump on Calin Travers.

Millie was still struggling on the floor; he could see her out of the corner of his eye and again anger surged through him. He gritted his teeth and came to his feet. The hardcase was laughing at him but he barely heard it through the blood pounding in his temples.

The hardcase grabbed him again. Calin swore his feet dangled off the floor.

'Nothin' personal, little girl.' The hardcase's breath smelled raw, like a skunk had crawled into his mouth and pissed all over his tongue. 'We all got our jobs to do, eh?'

'Jobs?' Calin echoed. A table was next to them. On the table was a heavy mug of beer and Calin's hand edged toward it. He wasn't going to beat this man with fists alone and all honor had gone out the batwings the moment the man sucker-punched him.

'A man told me this would help you recollect . . .'

What the hell did that mean? Calin wondered, but got no time to think on it.

Calin's fingers wrapped around the mug handle. He gave the hardcase a small grin.

The hardcase's brow crinkled. 'What the hell you smilin' for, you little horsechip? You simple or somethin'?'

Calin swung the mug.

A clunk sounded, heavy, ringing, as the glass bounced off the hardcase's temple. The man stood stock still, didn't even blink.

Calin hit him again.

The man dropped Calin, who staggered back a step.

The attacker stood still another moment, then Calin poked a finger against the man's chest. The hardcase went straight over backward and hit the floor in a cloud of sawdust on his back. He didn't move.

'Judas Priest . . .' mumbled Calin, setting the mug on the table.

The bartender came from around the bar and walked over to them.

'Thanks for all your help, Clive,' Calin said to him, frowning.

Clive shrugged. 'Was gonna haul out the shotgun if things got any worse, Calin.' The barkeep was a heavyset man, who appeared greasy from sweating continually.

'How the hell could they get any worse 'less he killed me?'

The barkeep shrugged again. 'You kill 'im?'

Calin gazed down at the unconscious hardcase. 'Sure as hell doubt it. The guy's strong as a goddamned bull.'

Three mintucs later, when the hardcase's eyes blinked open, Calin was sitting atop his chest, his Peacemaker jammed to the man's forehead.

'You and I are going to have a little parley, friend. I'm going to ask you some questions before the sheriff hauls your sorry ass off to a cell, and you'll answer them, because right now I'm paining all over and I got a hankerin' to pull the trigger and save the town the cost of puttin' you up for a couple days. You understand the rules?'

The hardcase blinked. 'I understand. It was just a job, nothin' against you, little girl.'

Calin clacked the man in the teeth with the Peacemaker's barrel. The man uttered a curse and blood streamed from his mouth.

'I'm not particularly partial to name-callin'. You best keep that in mind.'

The man remained silent, but fury swarmed in his eyes.

'Let's try this again with a little more respect, shall we? Why did you attack me?'

'Like I said, just a job. Was supposed to beat the hell out of you so you'd remember something.'

'Remember what?'

'Dunno.'

'Who hired you?'

'Dunno.'

'What the hell do you mean you don't know? You

don't know who hired you to beat the hell out of me?'

'Was dark. Got the notion he might have been an Injun, though.'

'An Injun? I've got no beef with any red man. Where you s'posed to meet him after you finish this job?'

'Meet him?'

'He's gotta pay you, right?'

'Paid in advance. In my top pocket.'

Calin, with his free hand, fished in the man's shirt pocket and pulled out a wad of greenbacks. He fanned them, counting fifty bucks.

'That's quite a piece of change for one beatin', isn't it?'

'I don't look a gift horse in the hindquarters. I didn't want the job when he told me who it was. Thought you were s'posed to be a tough *hombre*. You ain't so tough after all.'

Calin smirked. 'Says the fella flat out on the floor with me sittin' atop him.'

The hardcase frowned. 'You got a point. You givin' me back my money?'

'What do you think?' Calin backed off the man, keeping the gun leveled on him. Across the barroom the batwings parted as the Bannerville sheriff entered. He surveyed the room, then came toward Calin.

Calin holstered his Peacemaker. 'Way I see it, fella, you failed in your job so you don't deserve the money. But I reckon Miss Millie could use it since you saw fit to knock her around in such an ungentlemanly fashion. Reckon you got no objections to that arrangement?'

The hardcase glared. The sheriff had his gun drawn and was motioning for the man to get to his feet.

'I'll see him to a cell, Calin,' the lawdog said. 'Need a statement from you when you get the chance.'

'Will do.' Calin went to Millie and passed her the wad of greenbacks. She smiled, dragged her fingers down his shirtfront.

'You gotta go off so soon, Calin? Least I could do is give you your money's worth.'

He laughed, but it made his face hurt. 'Reckon all I want tonight is a soft bed and plenty of whiskey. You buy yourself something nice with that as a thank-you for being the only one in here who tried to save my ass.'

'Aw, Calin,' the barkeep said. 'Don't take it personal. We were too surprised to move. Your beer's on the house.'

He looked at the 'keep and nodded. 'It damn well ought to be.'

Calin grabbed his hat from the counter, then headed out through the batwings. He trudged back to his office, a sobering concern washing over him. Someone, possibly an Indian, had hired a man to beat him half to death to make him remember something. Remember what? The whole thing was puzzling and he got the notion that the hardcase

32

wasn't the end of it. Someone had a grudge, and a damn peculiar one at that. How was he going to go about finding out who? He might simply have to wait until the person struck again.

He groaned. Dammit, every inch of his body felt as if a stage had run over it. He had all he could do to cross the wide rutted main street and step on to the opposite boardwalk. The only consolation was he knew the pain would be a hell of a lot worse tomorrow morning after everything stiffened up.

He reached his small office and noticed a lamp still burning within. After entering, he plucked his hat from his head and tossed it on to a wallpeg to his left.

The office was small, but comfortable, with a couple of big leather chairs and two desks of dark wood. A young man sat at one, a stack of paperwork before him. The man wore spectacles and was balding, had sharp features.

'Horace, what the devil you still doing here? I told you to go home when it got dark.'

The man shrugged. 'Wanted to finish looking over these cases, but it might not matter. Figure I know where you'll be headed next. Say, what happened to you? You look like hell.' The secretary's brow furrowed.

Calin went to one of the big leather chairs and dropped into it, sighing. 'Bullfight at the saloon.'

'Bullfight?'

'Some fella strong as one tried to beat the hell out of me.'

Horace's face pinched. 'Why? Not that you lack for getting on some folks' bad side.'

Calin ignored the remark. 'Said someone hired him to do it, to make me remember something but I have no idea what he was talking about. Like you said, I got enemies. Manhunters always do, but something about this is just . . . I don't know. It gives me a bad feeling in my gut.'

'Where's this bull?' The secretary leaned back in his chair.

'Sheriff's entertaining him, but he's just hired meat. Doubt he knows anything other than what he's already told me.' Calin noticed the secretary staring at him. 'Why you looking at me that way?'

'Nothing, just never saw you take a beating before.'

Calin nodded, features darkening with an old memory. 'I took one once . . . swore it'd never happen again. Guess I was wrong. What'd you mean about knowin' where I'm going next, anyway?'

The secretary leaned forward, rummaged through the papers on his desk and located a yellow telegram slip. He got up and walked over to Calin, passed him the message.

'This came for you earlier. Telegraph man delivered it on his way home.'

Calin's gaze settled on the slip:

NEED YOUR HELP STOP COME TO SUN-
DOWN AT EARLIEST CONVENIENCE STOP
MARSHAL HANK TOMPKINS STOP

The dark feeling that had started earlier strengthened at the mention of the town on the slip. Sundown. He had been brought up there, lived there up until ten years ago, and not a pleasant memory came with the place. He had run into Tompkins a few times over the years; they'd ridden together on a couple cases. So Tompkins was marshal of Sundown now. . . .

'You're from Sundown, aren't you?' Horace asked as he reached his desk and sat again.

Calin nodded. 'Wasn't plannin' on ever goin' back there. But if Tompkins is askin' for my help he must really need it. Never rode with a better man.'

'So you're going?'

Calin sighed. Although he had little desire to return to that town and dredge up old ghosts, he owed the marshal there his life. On one of their cases Hank Tompkins had circled around to stop a man on a rooftop from shooting Calin in the back while he was confronting another outlaw.

'I'd rather stay around and try to figure out who wanted me to take a beating, but, yeah, I reckon I'm going. I'll ride out in the morning if I'm not too sore to get out of bed. All I want to do tonight is spend time with Doc Orchard . . .'

CHAPTER THREE

Sundown, Colorado, had changed little since the day Calin Travers rode out, ten years ago. Oh, perhaps the town itself had become more sprawling, gaslights had been installed and a railroad track snaked along its east end, but seeing it again unearthed the same feelings he'd experienced upon leaving: dread, remorse, guilt. He hadn't really expected anything different; some memories couldn't be wiped away, even with the passage of time, and he had to admit that when he'd left he'd left with things unfinished. Despite the years of building himself into the man he wanted to be, a man who wasn't a coward and didn't run from responsibilities or threats, the memories riding into this town dredged up made him wonder if he had come any distance in that respect at all.

Are you still a coward? Do you still want to turn around and ride back to Bannerville and never look back?

He slowed his chestnut into a slow walk as he

entered the outskirts of the town, anxiety riding his nerves. He couldn't deny that the thought of just turning back wasn't attractive, but if he ever truly had a chance to exorcise his ghosts it would have to be done here.

A lot of time had passed. Things might well be different. The boys whom he had let run his life were men now and had likely matured. *He* had matured. He wasn't the same weak boy who'd surrendered himself to fear.

Are you sure about that?

As he rode deeper into the town, he noted a number of new hotels, saloons and businesses. That didn't surprise him. He recollected the handful of families who'd held sway in this town – the Creeds, the Bretts, the Parlimeaus, the Fosters, names he had little desire to dwell upon, and they certainly would have seized upon any opportunity for prosperity the railroad brought.

Despite his effort to suppress the memories the names unearthed, a certain emptiness washed over him.

His gaze drifted up and over. In the distance, just beyond the town's northern wooded border, he imagined he could see the creek flowing through a clearing in those woods. Blood Creek. Called such because its heavy red clay content sometimes made the waters appear the color of old blood, the image of it conjured even darker memories, crippling regrets.

He shook off a case of the chills, though the air

was warm on this late-spring day.

You shouldn't have come here.

He could have stayed in Bannerville, concentrated on finding whoever had hired the hardcase to attack him last night. Why hadn't he? True, he owed Tompkins, but he suspected there was more to it than that. Maybe he'd been a man seeking redemption for too long and maybe the coward inside him was tired of shivering like a child afraid of the dark.

He shifted in the saddle, sore in too many places to count and burdened by the leaden emotion in his soul. It was too late to turn back. He was here and that was that.

He drew a long breath, calming himself. He told himself this was simply another mission. He would go through with it, his misgivings be damned.

Before leaving Bannerville at false dawn he'd checked in with the sheriff. He'd learned that his attacker had spent most of his time cursing the town, Calin, and cold beans he'd choked down for breakfast, but had offered nothing further about whoever might have hired him. The sheriff planned to hold on to the outlaw, so that little mystery could wait until he helped Tompkins out with whatever it was he needed.

Squaring his shoulders, he peered at the boardwalks. A few early risers with sleepy half-drawn eyelids and yawning mouths wandered towards their destinations. No one gave him even a passing look or appeared to recognize a prodigal son. For that he was just as glad.

He urged the chestnut to the left and reined up. A large window bore the legend MARSHAL'S OFFICE in arcing gilt lettering. He swung from the saddle, then tied the reins to the hitchrail.

After crossing the boardwalk to the door, he entered the office. As Calin closed the door, a man looked up from behind a desk. Tompkins was slim of build with a receding hairline that made him look twenty years older than Calin instead of ten. The lawdog's face showed the weathering of too many days on the trail. Tompkins had worked as a for-hire range detective most of his days, which was how he and Calin originally crossed paths. Calin, doing freelance work for a few spreads Tompkins had signed on with, had ridden with the man on a number of tough cases.

'Jesus H. Christ, as I live and breathe!' Tompkins sprang from his chair and came around the desk. 'Calin Travers – never thought I'd see the day you'd come back to this town.'

Calin was about to answer he'd thought the same thing, but his gaze followed a sound from the back, where three cells lined the rear wall. In one cell, a man sat on a bunk, knees drawn up to his chin, arms wrapped about his shins. A wild look showed in the man's eyes, a look that said the fellow was somehow trapped in the prison of his own mind. He appeared a wreck, hair disheveled, face drawn and gaunt, but Calin recognized him all the same.

'Christ, Foster . . .' he mumbled. A peculiar feeling of – what? Destiny? Fate? washed over him. Akin to the dread he'd felt the previous night after the attack, but stronger, more acute this time. Like pieces of some dark puzzle locking into place. Dark and deadly. He didn't care for the feeling one bit.

'Calin?' Tompkins's voice penetrated his reverie and he blinked, seeing the other man standing before him. 'You awright?'

'Huh?' he said, shaking off the cobwebs. 'Oh, yeah, Hank, sure. Just, just a rough night last night and my head's still a bit fuzzy.'

The marshal looked Calin over top to bottom, brow crinkling, eyes becoming serious. 'What the devil happened to you? You got more bruises on your face than I seen on a man thrown from a bronc. Get caught in a stampede?'

'Something like that. Just some unfinished business I'll need to attend to when I get back to Bannerville.'

'Well, hell, pull up a seat and sit a spell. Been what – going on five years since we last rode together?'

Calin nodded and grabbed a hardbacked chair while the marshal went back around his desk and lowered himself into his seat.

'That's about right, best I recollect.' Calin sat and doffed his hat, tossed it on to the desk. 'Was on the Henkins cattle-rustling case. You saved my life on that one, way I recall it.'

'Pshaw!' Tompkins waved off the notion. 'You'da

come out on top anyway.'

'Not with a bullet in my back, Hank. Never saw that other fella up on the rooftop.'

'You were one of the finest manhunters I ever seen, Calin. You'da found a way. I did nothing.'

'You always were too damn modest for your own good, Hank. Man needs just the right partner on tough cases and you were the best.'

Tompkins smiled, made a swipe at an imaginary strand of hair on his forehead. He leaned back a bit in his chair. 'Just doin' my job.'

Calin laughed. 'Reckon we had more folks doing their job the way you did we'd rid the West of outlaws. How long you been marshal in this town? Didn't think you were the type to settle in one place.'

The lawdog chuckled, held up his left hand to show Calin the gold band circling his ring finger. 'Didn't think so either till Sheila came along. Got myself hitched to the goddamnedest woman you ever met, but she wasn't about to put up with a man who spent more time on the trail than at home. So I signed on to this job two years ago and bought myself a small spread just west of town. Don't regret a single minute, though. Thought I would, but the right woman has a way of puttin' what's truly important into perspective. Say, 'bout time you found yourself a gal, ain't it?'

'Me?' Calin scoffed. 'What woman would have a restless sonofabitch like me?'

Tompkins cocked an eyebrow. 'Still got that

41

wanderlust in your blood, I see.'

'Wouldn't exactly call it wanderlust, but something won't let me settle down, least not yet.'

The marshal peered intently at him. 'You always rode with a ghost, Calin. Was hoping the next time I saw you that ghost would have stopped haunting you.'

'You got an eye for readin' men, Hank. But I doubt some ghosts ever go away.'

'No good comes from clinging to the past, Calin. Whatever it is that's got you by the balls, don't let it keep squeezing. One day you'll wake up and look back and your life will be wasted.'

Calin laughed, but the expression held a note of unease. 'Marriage turned you into a philosopher?'

'No, it's turned me into a realist. Like I said, gave me perspective.'

'Reckon I could use a measure of that.'

'So what the hell brings you back to Sundown, Calin? I reckon this ain't entirely a social call.'

Calin's brow furrowed and he studied the marshal for signs of a jest. 'I reckoned *you* did, Hank.'

'*I* did?' Puzzlement jumped on to the marshal's features.

Calin reached into his shirt pocket and pulled out the yellow slip of paper. 'You sent this, didn't you?' He tossed the paper on to the desk.

Hank Tompkins picked it up, scanned the lines. 'No, not me, though it sure as hell's got my name on it.'

'You're serious? You didn't send it?' Calin frowned, wondering just what the hell was up.

'No, but I reckon I'll take advantage of it. I'm working on a case that's got me buffaloed. If you're inclined to stay a spell I sure could use your help. You always were right good at putting facts together when they seemed unrelated. You were the better detective by far.'

Calin took the telegram back and stuffed it into his breast pocket. What the hell was going on here? First the attack in the saloon last night, now a telegram calling him back to this town from a friend who hadn't sent it.

'Someone's pulling my reins, Hank. I don't like the way things appear headed.'

'You reckon this has something to do with the unfinished business that put those bruises on your face?'

'Can't see a connection yet, but my gut tells me there's a thread somewhere that needs pullin'.'

Tomkins nodded. 'Your gut was usually right on the mark. Swear that manhunter's sixth sense of yours was some kind of supernatural thing.'

'Reckon it's more just reading the signs, even the ones that aren't always obvious.'

'We'll find out who sent that telegram. Don't cotton to folks using my name if they're up to no good.'

Calin nodded, pondering the situation and finding he had nothing more than vague dark feelings linking seemingly unconnected events. 'Your case, does it have something to do with that man in the cell?' Calin glanced back at the fellow, who hadn't moved. He was babbling under his breath, swaying on the cot.

'You know him?'

Calin nodded. 'Jim Foster. Used to know him when I lived here, least thought I did until . . . well, his family was well-to-do, one of the powers in this town.'

'Jim shunned his folks, least for the past few years. He became kind of a recluse, except for his blacksmithing work. Married himself a former bargirl. His family moved off after the old man passed. Far as I know they had no contact after that.'

'What's wrong with him? He looks . . .'

'Insane? That he is. Reckon any man would be after what happened to him.'

Calin glanced at Foster again, who seemed to be peering at him, but was more likely just looking straight through him, then looked back to Tompkins. 'What happened?'

'Hope you got a strong stomach because it ain't goddamn pretty. Best I can piece together he came home from his job two days ago and was forced to watch his wife murdered. Somebody skinned her alive and hung her hide out to dry on the fence post.'

'Christ . . .' Calin whispered, his belly sinking. 'What kind of fiend would do something like that?'

'If I didn't know better I'd say it was the work of

Injuns, but no Injuns 'round these parts for the past few years, except Old Sam and a younger guy name of Joe Sunkiller. Can't see how's the Fosters would have had any contact with either of 'em.'

'Injuns . . .' Calin's voice lowered. That was the second time in two days he'd heard that word and it didn't settle well, though for what reason he wasn't certain.

Or do you know a reason, Calin? Do you see the threads twining together?

'Calin?'

'Yeah?' He realized he had drifted off and Tompkins was staring at him again.

'You seem a mite more distracted than I recall from our days together.'

'Just . . . sickened, I reckon. Always am when I think of the atrocities one man can commit on another. Something like this . . .' He glanced at Foster, a great sorrow rising for him, despite the fact the last time they had crossed paths it had been less than amicable. 'Something like this is the work of a madman.'

'Inclined to agree, but that ain't the worst of it. 'Foster had a child, eight years old, I think.'

Dread tightened in Calin's throat. 'Oh, no . . .'

'Don't know yet. At the moment she's just missing and Foster's too buried in his own mind to say anything about what might have happened to her. If he saw anything it's locked in his head.'

Calin drew deep breath. He had seen things in his career, seen the evil of which men were capable, but this . . . this went beyond human. 'Any leads to the killer?'

Tompkins shrugged. 'None I could find at the cabin. Too much blood everywhere and Foster tracked it all over the place blindly before he came running into town screeching his lungs out. Always the chance he went plumb loco and did the deed himself, but I got a notion that ain't the case.'

'Marshal's sixth sense?' Calin ran a finger over his upper lip. He'd worked cases where men had murdered their wives. It wasn't out of the realm of possibility and such a brutal display pointed to an emotional connection or crime of passion.

'No, just that I found pieces of rope and some spikes pounded into the floor of his cabin. Looks like Foster was tied to the sofa and made to watch. Chewed his way through a rope, best I could tell. Plus three other men experienced the same thing in surrounding towns.'

'What?' Shock washed over Calin's face. 'You're telling me this wasn't an isolated incident?'

Tompkins shook his head. 'These other three, they all discovered their wives skinned alive, the hides hung either on hitchrails or fence posts. In two cases the homes had been burnt to the ground. These men lost everything they had. None of 'em, from what I can tell, are in their right minds anymore, though none is as bad off as Foster there.' Tompkins ducked his chin at the man curled up on the cot. 'They'll all have nightmares the rest of their born days, I imagine.'

'That points to a motive and pattern, a killer seeking revenge.'

'I figured as much. Whoever did this is either plumb loco or has some powerful grudge against these men. But I haven't found much of a connection between the men other than the fact they all came from Sundown and from affluent families.'

A dark suspicion made Calin's heart thud a beat faster. 'You got a list of the names?'

Tompkins nodded, pulled open a drawer and located a sheet of paper, then passed it to Calin.

Calin scanned the names on it and the suspicion became solid. 'Jesus . . .' he whispered, the threads drawing together a bit tighter.

'You know them?'

He frowned, nodded. 'I know them. These men, well, they were more boys when I knew them, but they all kept together, like a pack of coyotes. Reckless sorts, aware of their parents' power and influence in town and not afraid to flaunt it. They knew no one would touch them whenever they got into trouble. Most of it was minor, prank stuff. Foster, he tried to steal a cow once as a joke, but nearly got his ass blown off.'

Tell him the rest, Calin. Tell him what that dark suspicion in your mind is suddenly screaming. . . .

Not yet. Not until he was positive. He might be jumping to conclusions, forming a link where there was only coincidence.

'Got the notion there's something you're leaving out, Calin.'

47

Tompkins peered closely at him.

'You read me well as you always did, Hank. But I ain't quite ready to connect the dots yet.'

'When you do . . .'

'You'll be the second to know.' He gave Tompkins a weak smile. 'You got any leads on the little girl?'

'Not a one. Whoever took her stashed her somewhere or killed her and buried the body where we ain't likely to ever find it.'

'Anyone new in town?'

The marshal shrugged. 'Not recent. Sunkiller came in 'bout a year back. Don't know his background.'

'When did these killings start?' Calin passed the paper back to the marshal, who stuffed it back into the drawer.

'The first was four months ago.'

'Like to talk to this Sunkiller at some point.'

' 'Cause he's a Ute?'

' 'Cause he's the last stranger, though it's stretching it,' he said honestly, but couldn't deny that the tenuous connection to a time fifteen years ago, which led back to Indians, had to be investigated.

'Has a small shack on Jasper, north edge of town. But he spends most of his time at the Bullwhip saloon.'

Calin paused, thoughts returning to the list of names Tompkins had shown him. 'There was a fifth boy, used to lead the others, name of Jared Brett.'

Tompkins's eyebrow cocked. 'Brett? Really? He's still in town. Has a nice big house over on the west side. His family passed on a few years back and left him enough money so's he doesn't do much more than drink and keep that showpiece wife of his.'

Calin nodded, little surprised. 'Brett was always the worst of 'em. He . . . he saw things different. Figured the world owed him. And figured he could just take whatever he wanted.'

'Then he hasn't changed a lick. His parents' money bought him out of a pile of trouble over the years. Keeps cleaner now since I took over 'cause he knows his money means horsedung to me.'

'I'm guessing from the pattern I'm starting see with these murders it won't buy him out of the trouble he's got comin' his way.'

'What about you? You reckon this fella might be after you, since you got attacked 'fore coming here and someone went to the trouble of bringin' you back to Sundown?'

Calin's belly cinched. 'The thought occurred to me. Someone wanted me here, though I can't put together the why of it just yet. I was friends with these five for a brief time, but it ended . . . poorly.'

'Care to tell me about it?'

Calin uttered an uneasy chuckle. 'Not ready to confess my sins quite yet, Father Tompkins.'

Tompkins grinned. 'You always were a sarcastic sonofabitch, weren't you?'

'Some things never change.'

'Reckon they don't.'

'I'd like to try talking to Foster in his cell, you don't mind . . .'

Tompkins shrugged. 'Makes no nevermind to me. Can't see what good it's going to do you, though. He's not comin' back.' The marshal reached back into his desk and pulled out a key ring. He tossed it to Calin, who caught it as he stood.

'Obliged.'

'I got some errands to run. Lock him up when you're done and toss the key back in the desk, if you'd be so kind.'

'Will do.'

After the marshal left Calin walked over to the cell and studied the man on the cot for what seemed like an eternity, a mêlée of feelings swarming within him. Sympathy, sadness, even anger left over from a day long past.

He unlocked the door and stepped into the cell. Foster didn't acknowledge his entry.

Calin squatted in front of the bunk, peering into the man's eyes.

'Jim . . .' he said in a soothing voice. 'You recollect me?'

Jim Foster didn't stop swaying. His mumbling increased.

'It's Calin Travers. We used . . . to be friends of a sort once. Who did this thing to your wife, Jim? Tell me. I'll find him and make him answer for it.'

Foster's swaying became more agitated. Drool

ran from the corner of his mouth. 'Creek . . .' he mumbled, the word barely distinguishable.

A chill slithered down Calin's spine. 'What? What did you say?'

'Creek . . .' whispered Jim. 'Blood Creek . . . the Injuns, they go round and round, through the town . . . Blood Creek, no speak, round and round . . .' The words deteriorated into a jumble of sounds that carried no coherency.

Calin straightened, then backed from the cell and closed the door. He locked the cell, watched Jim Foster rock back and forth on the cot.

You've almost got it, haven't you, Calin? You can almost fit the pieces together and come up with part of the answer. . . .

Blood Creek. The names on the list. Indians. Fifteen years ago.

Something from the past had returned to strike at these men, something raging and violent and hungry for vengeance. But who? And why had it waited so long?

Whoever it is knows about you, too, Calin. That's why you were called back to Sundown. That's why you were attacked last night. Someone wanted you to remember that day at the creek.

But no one else had been at the creek that day, no one except these men whose wives had been murdered, and Jared Brett.

Yet there had to be someone else, someone who had waited to strike and instead of killing these men had chosen to take everything that meant something to them and leave them to suffer.

But you don't have a wife and possessions, do you, Cann? All you've got is your life. . . .

CHAPTER FOUR

The Bullwhip saloon opened early for breakfast, but by the time Calin paid the livery man a week in advance to board his chestnut, then secured a spot at the Black Horse Hotel and tucked his gear in a room, the noon sun hung brassy and high. Under a sapphire sky the day had grown warmer and the air smelled of dung and horse piss mixed with the fragrance of the fresh-cut spring flowers adorning a number of the shops. A line of sweat beaded on his brow beneath the rim of his Stetson.

Despite the bright day he couldn't shake the dread that had begun with last night's attack in Bannerville and strengthened after discovering he'd been called here on a ruse and learning of the murders.

Four murders. Each woman skinned alive. Four men who used to run together like a band of boy outlaws. Four men, one hopelessly insane in the marshal's jail, the others suffering the loss of what they held most dear.

A fifth man, Jared Brett, who, if Calin's suspicions

held true, was next on the list. Or, more accurately, Brett's wife.

And, last, the sixth man at the creek that day: himself. Fifteen years ago he'd been a starry-eyed boy, one who'd reckoned everything important came with being a part of that gang of ruffians. But one who never truly fit in. He wasn't like Brett and his hellions, no matter what a juvenile's misguided notions had told him. He'd discovered that soon enough, and had run. Like a coward.

Another person had been at the creek that day. Someone innocent, someone who had never suspected just what those boys were capable of.

Is that why he really wanted to talk to this Joe Sunkiller? Because of a Ute girl whose name he didn't know to this day, whose purity he couldn't save and for whom he still felt somehow responsible?

Just because Sunkiller was an Indian . . . well, it might mean nothing. He might be grasping for something, anything, because of a gut feeling hung on a coincidence. But he'd broken cases in the past by relying on that manhunter's sixth sense, and frankly he had little else to go on, other than questioning Jared Brett. He'd get to that soon enough, though the prospect didn't thrill him.

Still, he couldn't discount the fact that a man had been hired by an Indian to attack him, nor the killings . . . he'd seen the results of a Comanche attack once, years back; it was every bit as brutal as these deaths. That, combined with what had happened to that Ute girl, gave him pause.

If this Sunkiller had no connection to the case, Calin reckoned he'd be able to determine that easily enough. He had a good eye for spotting liars and lots of practice in his line of work.

He pushed through the batwings, doffed his hat and stood on the landing, surveying the barroom. The saloon itself looked the same as a hundred others he'd been in from Colorado to Texas. A long bar, chipped and scuffed, ran along the north wall, and stairs at the back led to upper rooms where girls of the line plied their trade. A piano rested against the wall to the left and sunlight beamed in dusty shafts through the large front window.

The place was deserted except for a barkeep, a heavyset man with a beard that dangled to his barrel chest, standing behind the bar, leaning on the counter, and one other man, an Indian with shoulder-length hair and a black duster, who sat at a back table. The man's hat rested on the table next to a bottle of whiskey.

Tompkins's prediction that Joe Sunkiller could be found at the saloon had proved accurate. As Calin studied him, a peculiar winsome expression spread over Sunkiller's lips. The Indian's dark eyes locked with Calin's. A slight chill trickled down his back, despite the warmth of the day. Perhaps the stretch was not quite so far, he thought suddenly. An air of darkness seemed to hang about the man.

Calin took the three stairs down to the saloon proper. As he approached the table, Joe Sunkiller didn't avert his gaze. He merely watched Calin with a look that said he'd expected the visit, if not at this moment, then at some point soon.

'You Joe Sunkiller?' Calin asked.

'You come to watch the dime-novel Injun drinking his firewater, Mr Travers? I hear it's big sport in these parts. Watch the lowly red man piss away his life and mourn for those days of old when we rode barebacked across the wild range, the wind in our hair, fire in our blood.' He laughed, took a swig from the bottle.

Calin frowned. He didn't know quite what he had expected out of Joe Sunkiller, but that wasn't it. 'That's a damn peculiar way of greetin' a fella.'

Sunkiller's eyebrow lifted. 'You reckon? I don't. It's what's expected. Why not play to it? Maybe before you leave you can toss some silver in my hat.'

'You don't talk much like an Indian.'

Sunkiller chuckled without humor. 'And what should an Indian talk like, Mr Travers? Like those of your white man's dime novels? Sorry, make heap big mistake.'

'That's not what I meant. I reckon you talk more educated than many of the whites I meet in these parts.'

A distant look drifted across Sunkiller's eyes. 'I had a lot of time to learn proper English, not that I bother using it all the time. When it suits me.'

'It suits you now?'

'You have a reason for seeking me out?' Sunkiller asked, ignoring the question.

Calin indicted a chair. 'Mind?'

'Suit yourself.' Sunkiller ducked his chin at the chair and Calin sat, placing his hat on the table.

'How'd you know who I am?' Calin leaned back in the chair, folded his arms.

'I've seen your likeness in the papers. You have quite a reputation in this town.'

'Some towns only embrace you once you've made a name for yourself.'

Sunkiller nodded. 'Or become infamous.'

'That apply to you?' Calin asked outright. 'You lookin' to become infamous?'

The Indian laughed again, an expression that made Calin suddenly wonder from its complete lack of emotion who was the more detached from reality, Sunkiller or the man sitting in the marshal's cell.

'That funny somehow?' Calin asked when Sunkiller didn't answer.

'No, Mr Travers, I am not looking to become infamous. I am not looking to become anything other than what I am.'

Calin wasn't liking the darkness he saw in the man's eyes. Something was wrong with Sunkiller. He'd seen the look before, in the eyes of outlaws, killers. 'And just what are you?'

Sunkiller's expression sobered. 'What exactly are you asking me, Mr Travers?'

Calin leaned forward, set both elbows on the table. 'I've never been right good at beating around the bush, so I'll put it to you straightlike: Four women are dead in these parts, skinned alive. Those women's husbands have a connection in their past and at the moment that's all I can see linking the murders. You got a notion who these men are?'

A fleeting smile touched Sunkiller's lips. 'I know them. Everybody in Sundown does. I have heard of the murders.'

There was more to it; Calin heard it in the man's voice. 'You have anything to do with them?'

Sunkiller's eyes narrowed, a flash of anger crossing them. 'Why? Because I'm an Injun? Because you need somebody to blame and I'm the only red man in these parts?'

Calin ignored the man's sarcasm. 'There's another, I hear tell.'

'Old Sam? I doubt eighty-year-old men have much motive for butchering women in the old way.'

'Old way?'

'Oh, don't you read your dime novels, Mr Travers? We're no better than beasts. You see, Injuns don't just scalp folks, they take their hides and wear them as trophies.'

'That ain't the least bit funny, Sunkiller.' Calin's brow furrowed. 'Reckon I don't give a damn what you think my motives might be for asking you questions. Only thing I care a lick about is finding a little girl and punishing the monster who took the lives of those women and left their menfolk suffering the way Jim Foster is, in a cell at the marshal's.'

Sunkiller remained quiet a moment, gulped another swig of his whiskey, then stood. He grabbed his hat, set it on his head and peered down at Calin.

'These men you speak of . . . are they godly men, Mr Travers? Are they without sin?'

'Just what the hell is that supposed to mean?'

Sunkiller smiled a lifeless smile, then started walking away, grabbing the bottle from the table as he did so. He paused on the top step of the landing and turned his head to look back at Calin. 'You feel pity for these white women, Mr Travers, do you not? Yes, I see it in your eyes. Regret. Sympathy. Sorrow. But would you feel the same for a red woman? Would you honor her memory and avenge the sins committed against her, the way you do with these others?'

Calin's head lifted, green eyes narrowing. 'I usually get a feeling about the men I question, Sunkiller. I figure they're either lying to me or they ain't.'

Sunkiller's expression remained placid. 'And what feeling do you have about me, Mr Travers?'

'I'm not getting the feeling you ain't lyin' . . .'

The smile came back to Sunkiller's face, then he turned and pushed through the batwings out into the day.

Calin watched the batwings swing, running his finger over his upper lip. The feeling he'd gotten from that man . . . he didn't like it one damn bit. He got the odd notion Sunkiller might be two people, one who pretended to be a cat playing with a mouse and another darker soul, barely restrained within. Perhaps the man had only been a little drunk and was simply releasing pent-up bitterness, but Calin bet there was more to it.

While he had no real evidence linking the man to the murders, he couldn't deny the suspicion that if he sought a murderer he need look no further than the man who'd just left the saloon.

You're making a big leap, aren't you?

Maybe. Maybe he was just getting worn out on all the death, and running and coming back to this town had increased those feelings.

'He has a woman . . .' A voice penetrated his reverie and he looked over to see the barkeep staring at him from behind the counter.

Calin stood, grabbed his hat, went to the bar and sat on a stool. 'Whiskey . . .' He reached into his pocket and pulled out a silver dollar, tossed it on to the counter.

The 'keep pushed himself away from the counter, grabbed a glass from beneath the bar and a bottle from the hutch. Calin glanced at his reflection in the cracked mirror behind the bar. A ghost peered back. He looked suddenly older, worn, and there were dark pouches beneath his eyes, lines on his face he swore hadn't been there a couple days ago. The bruises didn't help. Had coming back to Sundown done that to him? Christ, he'd only been back a few hours but somehow it felt as if he'd never left.

The 'keep slid the glass in front of him. He swallowed a long drink, letting the liquor burn its way down his throat. It tasted like cow piss and made his eyes water.

'Sunkiller has a woman?' he asked, setting the glass down.

The bartender nodded. 'Annette Pickler. She runs the general store. She might know more about him if you're lookin' for something.'

'You know who I am, I take it?'

'I know. Seen the papers, but recollect you from when you were a boy. Knew your pa 'fore he and your ma were . . .'

'That was a long time ago,' Calin said. Both his parents had perished shortly after his eighteenth birthday, killed by bandits as they rode a stage bound for relatives in Missouri. He'd been on his own ever since. The sympathetic look on the barkeep's face made Calin squirm on his stool.

'Reckon it was, but also reckon you never had it easy here. You went and made a name for yourself, though. Some of us here are damn proud of you, regardless of what you might think.'

Calin studied the man, noting sincerity. 'Reckon I appreciate the sentiment. Wasn't much you could do about those who ran this town back when I left.'

'Most are gone now, 'cept for that Brett. He's a goddamn waste of hide, if you ask me. Some of the others changed, 'specially Jim Foster. He always went around with that hangdog face, like somethin' was always pulling on his tail.'

'Reckon something was.' Calin couldn't keep the sarcasm out of his tone.

'You here to help him?'

Calin nodded. 'I'm here to help Tompkins, but it relates.'

'I recall they never got tired of taunting the hell out of you. Why would you bother riskin' your own hide for them?'

The same question had occurred to him earlier, though he'd not dwelled on it. 'Number of reasons, I suppose. Their women didn't ask for what happened to them and Foster's little girl's still missing.' Calin paused, looking for a deeper answer. 'And maybe because I got to pay penance for my own sins. I made a promise to myself years ago, that I had to do what I felt was right no matter what it cost me, even if it meant my life. Findin' that killer . . . it's right. No matter what kinda skunks Brett and his gang were, no matter how much they might deserve punishment for some of the things they did, they also deserve justice at the hands of the law, not some animal who butchers their women and takes their children.'

The 'keep peered at him, nodding slightly. 'Most folks figure something should have caught up with those boys way before now, 'specially Brett. He got away with whatever he wanted, right up till Tompkins came in.'

Calin uttered a lifeless laugh, mind drifting. 'Reckon I should have come back sooner, brought Brett in for something a long time ago. Maybe it would have prevented what's happening somehow. But I'm ashamed to admit I was afraid of him and the rest.'

'Lots of folks were and you were just a boy.'

Calin shrugged. 'Reckon I ain't no longer. It's time to make right an old wrong.'

'Ain't sure what you're referring to, Calin, but it's high time Brett faced up to his sins.'

'Brett . . .' Calin frowned. 'Sunkiller was right, wasn't he?'

' 'Bout what?'

'Don't matter the color of woman's skin. Justice can't close its eyes to one and not the other . . .'

Puzzlement creased the 'keep's forehead. 'Not sure I get where you're goin'.'

Calin smiled. 'Don't matter . . . Obliged for the whiskey.' He slid off the stool and began walking from the saloon.

'Calin . . .' the 'keep said behind him.

'Yeah?'

'Watch your back. I hear Sunkiller's got a powerful bad temper.'

'Hope that's the least I have to worry about with him.' Calin pushed through the batwings.

CHAPTER FIVE

A bell clinked above the door as Calin entered the general store fifteen minutes later. After shutting the door behind him he walked down an aisle of shelves lined with canned goods, jars of preserves and fruits and bins of penny candy. Sacks of flour and grain were piled on the floor. A woman looked up from behind the counter as he approached, her face soft, kind, but a little plain. Her dull brown hair was pulled back into a bun and her blue eyes appeared washed out, weary.

'Pleasant day to you, sir,' she said. She smoothed the front of her simple blue dress and gave him a warm smile. He noticed she was a bit plump of hip and bosom and carried a strained look that made her appear older than she likely was.

He tipped a finger to his hat brim and smiled back. 'Are you Annette Pickler?'

'I am. Do I know you?' Her brow crinkled and an odd look came into her eyes. Worry, maybe, but for what reason he couldn't guess.

His gaze went to a yellowish splotch on her jaw line, just below the ear.

'Where'd you get that?' He ducked his chin at the waning bruise, dispensing with any preliminaries or tact. What the 'keep had mentioned about Sunkiller's temper came to mind.

Her fingers, trembling slightly, went to the blemish. 'It's nothing really. Clumsy me, I ran into a door 'bout a week back . . .'

She was lying. The hesitation in her voice betrayed her. She hadn't run into a door, she had run into a fist. He let it slide for the moment, but it gave him a powerful reason to dislike Joe Sunkiller.

He glanced about, then back to her. 'You own this store?'

'Yes, yes I do. Is there something you need?' A fleeting note of pride came in her voice, mixed with sorrow, if he read her correctly.

'Unusual, I mean, for a woman to own a general store.' He tried to make the statement sound casual but he'd never really learned the art of small talk and he could tell Annette Pickler's guard was going up.

'It was my husband's . . . he died, in a bank hold-up a year ago.'

He nodded. 'Sorry to hear that, ma'am.'

'Just who are you, mister? Why are you askin' me questions?' Her face suddenly hardened and her voice had gone flat.

He removed his hat, held it before him, fingering the brim. 'My name's Calin Travers. I'm helping out the marshal on a case, some killings that occurred in these parts.'

He watched for her reaction closely and got exactly what he wanted. Fear. Or, more accurately, acute worry. Where Joe Sunkiller had been skilled at saying one thing while hiding another, this woman had no such talent. She wore her emotions on her sleeve and right now he could see she was chewing over something in her mind, something that was causing her distress.

'Terrible thing, those women dyin' that way . . .' Her voice wavered a bit.

'Reckon it certainly was, but I got a notion what you're sayin' isn't what you're thinkin'.'

The look in her eyes became one of near panic now, but she managed to keep control over it.

'I'm sure I don't know what you mean, Mr Travers. It was horrible, what happened to those women. I'm sure the marshal will find whoever's responsible and see to it justice is done.'

He was surprised at the sincerity in her voice. For a woman whom he felt sure was hiding something, she was a contradiction.

'You know a man name of Joe Sunkiller?'

Again fear swept across her blue eyes.

'He's . . . I spend time with him.'

'Might say he's your beau?'

Her head bowed and she stared at the spot on the counter, then looked back up at him. Something else was in her eyes now, something he couldn't read. 'We . . . we plan to marry in the summer.' Her tone carried none of the hope and excitement he might have expected from a bride-to-be.

'Why, ma'am?'

'Why?' A puzzled look crossed her face.

'Why would you marry someone who hits you?'

'I . . .' Her hand went back to the bruise, confirming his suspicion. 'I don't know what you mean.' Her voice hardened a measure. 'Frankly, it's none of your business, Mr Travers. Joe treats me well.'

'Does he?' He knew he had pushed her a bit too hard and perhaps lost the moment of opportunity for learning something pertaining to the case, if indeed she knew anything. It occurred to him he'd never spent much time around women except bargals and it was suddenly painfully obvious the techniques he was accustomed to using on men and outlaws didn't apply with the fair sex.

She averted her gaze, remained silent.

He set his hat back atop his head. 'You know anything about these murders or have any part in what happened, ma'am, you best talk to me about it 'fore you end up like those other women . . .' He hoped his tone came off as reassuring, friendly, but was afraid it sounded more like an accusation.

But maybe he was wrong because something else crossed her eyes then, something that said she was worried about that very thing. 'I—'

Whatever she was about to say ended abruptly with the clinking of the bell above the door. Calin turned to see a man standing in the entry, backlit by the sunlight streaming in from the street. Annette

Pickler uttered a small gasp and took a step back from the counter.

'You finished with your business here, Mr Travers?' Joe Sunkiller asked, starting down the aisle.

'Just checkin' on supplies, Sunkiller. Find I might be stayin' a spell.' Calin's gaze locked with the Indian's; he saw fury in the other man's eyes, some directed at him, some at the woman behind the counter.

'I reckon she doesn't need your business. Why don't you find what you need elsewhere?'

Travers gave him a frown. 'Why is it whenever I talk to you I get the notion you're speakin' out of two sides of your mouth?'

'Isn't that the way of the Injun, Mr Travers? Again I refer you to your dime-novel writers. They are known for their accuracy . . .'

Calin sighed. 'We'll talk again, Sunkiller. Reckon that's the one thing about you I'm sure about. I got a notion the next time it won't be so . . . cordial . . .'

Sunkiller's expression didn't change, nor did his gaze waver from Calin. 'Perhaps not . . .'

'Ma'am.' Calin tipped a finger to his hat, then walked down the aisle, swearing he could feel Sunkiller's gaze burning into his back. He'd gotten nothing tangible from Annette Pickler, but hoped she'd think over what he'd said, because if Sunkiller were involved, her own life might well be in danger.

Annette Pickler watched Calin Travers leave with a

surging fear in her belly. Joe was going to hit her again, she was sure. He would never believe she had said nothing to the man and would take out his anger on her, the way he had too many times before. She wished she could end it with him, but he frightened her in ways she couldn't even begin to speak of to the Travers man. Travers's thinly veiled accusations against Sunkiller had only made her more afraid, more worried that Joe was lying to her.

Her face tightened and she folded her arms across her bosom, summoning her courage. 'You promised me you found that little girl wanderin' in the woods outside of town.'

Joe Sunkiller smiled the smile of a snake. 'That what Travers was askin' you, 'bout that girl?'

'Not in so many words. But I reckon he thinks you got somethin' to do with those women who got killed, and that little girl, she was Foster's child.'

'Foster's in no condition to care for her, like I told you. We're doin' him a favor.'

'But the marshal's gonna be lookin' for her. Wouldn't it better if we just tell him she's all right—'

Sunkiller's face darkened. 'You best shut your mouth and forget what Travers said 'fore . . .'

Anger sparked in her eyes. ' 'Fore I end up like them? Like those murdered women?'

Sunkiller suddenly grabbed two handfuls of her dress at the bosom and yanked her over the counter. She bleated a sound of fear and she knew better, but couldn't stop herself. Any sign of weakness on her part only enraged him.

He hurled her into a shelf stacked with canned goods. Pain splintered across her back and cans tumbled from the shelf as she crashed down. One glanced off her skull and she felt a trickle of blood down the side of her face. Another crashed into her cheek, opening a small cut with its edge. She looked up, dazed.

'Please . . . please, Joe, tell me you didn't have nothin' to do with those poor women . . .' Her voice deteriorated into a jumble of pleas, pleas for him to tell her what she was becoming certain were lies but which would save her from his wrath and her own guilt. Because when it came down to it she was a coward, too afraid to go to the marshal with her suspicions, too afraid that Sunkiller would somehow know and kill her before she ever said a word.

'You got some goddamn nerve questioning me, Annette.' He leaned over, grabbed her dress again and hauled her to her feet. He jammed his lips against hers and she tried to resist. He pulled back, fury lancing his dark eyes. 'I told you to keep your mouth shut about that girl and you best do so. Things can get a hell of a lot worse if you betray me.'

She saw insanity in his eyes, then. She was used to fury, spite, bitterness, his all-too-often forays into himself where he just stared for hours, but this . . . this for the first time told her the man she had lain with, the man she planned to marry, might be something much worse than she'd ever dreamed, some-thing evil.

'I-I won't tell . . .' she mumbled, tears streaming from her eyes, unable to think of anything other than living through this moment, escaping his rage.

He jammed his lips against hers again, and she knew she had better respond, because if he suspected any reluctance on her part, any lie, she would pay dearly for it.

The bell above the door clinked and he pulled back. Two women had come in and were staring at them, a look of distress on their faces.

'She fell against the shelf,' Sunkiller said, smiling that ingratiating smile of his. 'I was helping her up, but as you can see she is a bit shaken.'

Neither woman looked particularly convinced, but Annette knew he wouldn't give a damn what they thought. He guided her to the counter, then left her to her customers. She watched him leave, wishing God would grant her the courage to put a knife in his back.

Jared Brett had inherited well. His house rose three stories and covered enough square feet to support a small town in Calin's estimation. A wide columned porch wrapped about its entire front and left side. The windows were double-sashed, twelve-paned. The white siding was scrubbed clean. He noted Eastlake style latticework, cutouts and spindles, expansive flower gardens, well-tended, bursting with spring color. The grounds were as groomed as a fella about to court the love of his life.

Calin reined up a hundred paces from the place, surveyed the area. His mind drifted back to the last time he had encountered Jared Brett. It was a few days before he'd left Sundown for what he thought was for good. Brett had picked another fight with him, sent him flying over a hitchrail into a puddle of horsedung and muck in full view of half the town, none of whom made a move to help him. Just another in a line of Brett's constant taunts after the incident at Blood Creek.

Brett always was the worst of the bunch, the meanest. He was no better than a hardcase of means, but a natural leader and the others followed him without question. Calin suspected they had been afraid of him, afraid he would do to them what he had done to Calin and others who refused to bend to his will.

Brett had stepped over the line too many times to count, not just that day at Blood Creek. Only his parents' wealth had kept the young renegade out of a jail cell.

Now Brett appeared to have everything. A fancy house, a showpiece wife and a life of luxury. When it came to fairness in this world sometimes the wicked got the better deal. But if whoever was after the boys had his way, Brett's marker was about to come due.

Calin shook his head, telling himself he was a fool for even bothering trying to warn Brett. If an innocent woman's life wasn't involved he might have seriously considered leaving Brett to his fate. But like he told the 'keep, he'd made a promise to himself to do what was right. But he reckoned sometimes forgiveness was harder to come by than justice and sometimes a man had to settle simply for upholding his convictions.

He gigged his horse into an easy gait until he reached the house. He dismounted, tethered the reins around a silver-plated hitchpost, then took the steps slowly to the porch. He couldn't deny the anxiety fluttering in his belly and the washed-out feeling flooding his legs. Old fears died hard and he didn't imagine Brett's reception would be cordial. With a steadying breath, he grabbed the gilt-plated knocker and banged on the door.

He found himself half-hoping Brett was not in, but a moment later the door opened. If his legs had felt unsteady before they now became more so for an entirely different reason.

A woman stood in the doorway. Her blonde hair framed a face that was one of the loveliest he had ever seen. Her nose was small, slightly turned-up and her high cheekbones were kissed with rose. Her full lips, slightly parted, were moist and inviting as a summer peach and her sapphire eyes promised a man Heaven, but with the penalty of Hell.

'Yes?' she said, voice lilting. Her blue eyes made him struggle to find his voice.

He noticed she wore a pink silk robe that lay open at the front, revealing far more of her ample bosom than was proper. As if she noticed her effect on him, she gracefully lifted an arm to grasp the door frame, revealing an even deeper glimpse of her treasures.

Calin Travers had never fainted before but in that instant he gave it serious consideration. He tried to get his mouth to work, but no sound came out.

She giggled angelically. 'You like what you see, mister? All fellas do.'

'Get the hell away from the door dressed like that, you sorry whore!' a voice snapped from within the mansion.

She laughed and pulled her robe shut.

The shout shook Calin loose of her spell and the seriousness of what he had come to the mansion for sobered him. 'I'm lookin' for Jared Brett . . .'

'That bear you just heard roar . . .' She gestured him inside, leaning back against the door so he had to turn sideways to get past her. He got a whiff of her flowery perfume, its scent intoxicating.

The foyer was elegant, with a marble floor and a crystal chandelier overhead. A huge staircase, with ornate banisters of rich dark wood, led to the second floor. To either side were huge double doors. The doors on the right lay open and led to a drawing-room.

The woman closed the front door, then indicated for him to follow her. He wasn't so impressed with the elegant surroundings to ignore the luxurious sway of her backside.

The drawing-room was more extravagant than the foyer, with velvet-cushioned, wingback chairs and sofas, a gold-trimmed ivory harpsichord in one corner and a mahogany bar running along one wall, upon which rested a silver humidor, crystal glasses and decanters filled with amber liquor. Blue velvet drapes hung on the double windows overlooking the front yard. Another chandelier glittered with the sunlight that streamed through those windows.

In the room, near the bar, a man sat in one of the large wingback chairs, like some sort of dung-gilded king on a velvet throne, a half-empty glass in one hand, a cigar in the other. The room stank of rich sweet smoke that made Calin's already nervous belly slightly nauseated. Seeing Jared Brett after all these years brought back a flood of memories, none of them good. Brett had intimidated him then, and maybe still did, despite his resolve not to take a backward step from Brett's type ever again.

Shaking off the momentary shock of seeing the man once more, he saw plainly that Jared Brett had done some changing over the years. Brett had been a wiry sonofabitch when they were teenaged boys, strong as any seasoned ranch hand, always eager and ready with a fist. Now he carried a good fifty pounds extra, most of it layered around his waist and hanging under his chin. The man's eyes were sunken, with dark half-circles beneath, his nose veined from too much drink. But one thing hadn't changed: the old arrogance still held sway in his manner. Calin could see that plainly in the look that crossed Brett's face upon seeing a ghost walk into his drawing-room.

'Jesus Christ . . .' Brett rose from his chair and set his cigar on a silver tray on the bar. His forehead knotted as he squinted and peered at Calin.

'Jared . . .' Calin forced his voice to remain steady, something that took every ounce of his control.

'Never thought I'd see your sorry ass back in Sundown, let alone my house.' Brett came up to him. Calin felt an urge to back up a step, the way he used to years ago, but held his ground. He was not a boy anymore. He'd spent enough of his young life afraid of Brett and he refused to give in to that fear now.

'Can't say I wasn't of the same notion, but times change and we end up doin' things we never thought we would.'

Brett laughed, a mocking sound. 'Do they change, Travers? You're still afeared of me, ain't you? I can see it in your eyes.'

Brett's wife, who had gone to the bar and poured herself a drink, giggled.

'What the goddamn hell you laughin' at, Sally Ann?' Fury flashed across Brett's eyes. Sally Ann Brett was mocking him and he didn't care for it, thought Calin. He noticed some kind of tension between them, in the way they looked at each other, the way her carriage became rigid at his challenge.

'Why, nothin', Jared.' Her voice was slightly slurred, he noticed now that he had recovered from his initial infatuation with the woman. 'I'd *never*

laugh at you, sugar. Just watchin' the cock fight . . .'
She went to one of the sofas and lowered herself
into it, her arm drifting up on to the back and the
front of her robe falling open again.

Calin wished he could force himself to look away.

Brett's face turned red. 'For chris'sakes, will you
close your robe. Have you no goddamn shame at
all?'

She smiled probably the nastiest smile Calin had
ever seen from a woman. 'Not since I married you
for your money, sugar.'

Brett's face went from red to purple. He glared at
her. 'How dare you act that way in front of a
stranger . . .'

She giggled and gazed at Calin, a mischievous
glint dancing in her eyes. 'Oh, I'm bettin' the
stranger likes the view just fine, don't you,
stranger?'

Brett appeared about to burst. He wanted to
strike out at something, but held it together for the
time being. 'I'll deal with you later, Sally Ann.' He
turned back to Calin and Calin pried his gaze from
Sally Ann's cleavage. 'What the hell'd you'd come
back to Sundown for, Calin? And why are you here,
in my house? You should have stayed gone. You
never belonged in this town.'

Calin folded his arms. 'Humbled as I am by your
welcome, Jared, I came to ask you some questions
about some killin's in these parts. I'm workin' with
the marshal.'

Jared laughed, a sound laced with spite and

77

mockery. 'I'd heard tell you'd become some big-name manhunter. I couldn't hardly believe a scared little runt like you chased down men for a livin'. Figured it was all horsedung make up by them writers.'

'Like I said, things change. Some things, anyway.'

'Watch your goddamned tongue, Calin. I can still beat the hell out of you.' The look on Brett's face told Calin he'd welcome the chance to do it, too. He was still angry with Sally Ann and it didn't matter where that anger landed.

Calin's eyes narrowed with a measure of resolve. He would not allow this man to intimidate him anymore. While he'd been nervous about confronting Brett after all these years, he saw now that the man was nothing more than a pathetic waste of a skin who'd created a hell of his own indulgences. For everything he had, he had nothing. Maybe there was a measure of justice in that somehow.

'Four men's wives have been killed, Jared. Skinned alive.' A small gasp came from Sally Ann Brett, but Jared's expression didn't change.

'That s'posed to concern me?' Brett's tone, if anything, was more belligerent.

'Reckon you know Jim Foster's sitting in the marshal's jail, out of his wits. The other three men all ran with you. Those fellas were all at Blood Creek that day . . .'

Fury flashed into Jared Brett's eyes with the mention of Blood Creek. He suddenly dropped the glass in his hand, then his arms pistoned out, slamming Calin flush in the chest and hurling him backward.

Calin, unprepared for the sudden push, went over a mahogany coffee table, a crystal vase with fresh flowers crashing to the floor with him.

He looked up to see Jared glaring, heard Brett's wife giggling again.

'You know goddamn better than to mention that day in front of anyone, Travers. I best not hear it again 'less you want it jammed down your throat.'

Calin took a deep breath, anger boiling in his veins. The time had come, hadn't it? All those years of fear, of taking Brett's taunts and all his training over the past ten years had come down to this confrontation.

They were no longer boys in their teens; they were men. A man didn't back away from his ghosts. And he didn't accept another's domination.

Gripping his composure, he brushed some of the broken glass from his sleeve as he came to his feet and faced Jared.

'I'm no longer a boy, Jared.' His voice came steady, determined. 'Fifteen years ago until the time I left Sundown you made my life a living hell. I was a coward, then. I ran from you and the others. I'm not runnin' anymore.'

Jared laughed. 'You ain't changed, Travers. No matter what the papers say about you now. You ain't changed. You were stupid going against me that day and you were stupid comin' here today thinkin' I give a damn what happened to Foster and the rest. Get the hell out of my house and never come back or next time I'll kill you, way I should have fifteen years ago.'

'No.' Calin's voice remained low, hard and for an instant Jared Brett seemed taken aback like mountain lion snapped at by a terrier.

Then fury overwhelmed the heavyset man and he made a grab for Calin's shirt. Calin was ready for him this time. His hands knifed up, slammed against the insides of Jared's wrists and snapped outward before Brett could get a grip. Jared hesitated, momentarily surprised by the move, perhaps a little too lubricated to react fast enough.

Calin refused to give him any time to recover. He slammed a fist into Jared's face; blood sprayed from Brett's nose. The heavier man bellowed and tried to swing but the extra weight and soft life had slowed him, made him clumsy. He was still powerful, no doubt, but he had to lay his hands on his opponent first to use that strength.

Calin sidestepped, jabbing a short punch into Brett's lower ribs. With the sound of a brittle crack, Jared roared. Calin couldn't deny a measure of satisfaction. That cracked rib would pain Jared for weeks.

Pivoting, Calin launched a sidekick into the same rib, landing flush. Jared gasped and his entire body quaked.

Calin arced a crisp right into the man's temple and Brett staggered.

Brett tried to right his balance, swing a stout arm. The blow would have taken Calin's head off had it connected, but he bobbed, ducking under it, then came up with an sharp uppercut that slammed into the heavier man's chin.

For a moment Calin lost control of his skills; every ounce of fury and repressed shame from those days long ago burst loose and drove him to throw punch after punch at the wavering man's face. Each blow landed with the sound of a gunshot. Each snapped Brett's head back and was met without resistance.

Jared Brett crumbled. He hit the floor like a tree falling and lay gasping. Sally Ann Brett kept laughing. Something about the sound was unnerving and brought Calin out of his possessed fury.

Calin bent over Brett, grabbed the man's shirt and hauled his face close. Blood streamed from Brett's nose and mouth and his eyes were glassy.

'Listen close, you sonofabitch. You ever lay a hand on me again and the next time I'll put a bullet in you. I came here to warn you, you stupid bastard. I got a strong notion those murders are somehow connected to all of us who were at Blood Creek that day and your wife might be next on the killer's list. You want her hide to end up hanging on your fence?'

Sally Ann Brett suddenly stopped laughing. 'What? What do you mean?'

Calin glanced at her. She had moved to the edge of the sofa, her robe hanging fully open. 'Whoever's after Jared and his friends is striking at them through their wives and their possessions. Reckon when he comes, he'll get you first.'

Her face sobered, fear flooding her eyes. 'You have to protect me. He won't.' She nudged her head at her husband.

Calin let Jared go and the man fell back, panting, but made no move to get up.

Calin, straightening, peered down at him. 'You best pray I find out who's doing this before he comes for you, Brett. 'Cause he'll take your wife and everything you own and you won't be able to stop him, not the pathetic way you are now.'

Brett's eyes cleared a measure. 'Go to hell, Calin. I don't need no sympathy from you.'

'It ain't sympathy. It's my job. Far as I'm concerned if it weren't for your wife I'd be inclined to let the sonofabitch have you.'

Jared's wife sprang off the sofa. She ran up to Calin, threw her arms around him, pressed her lips to his. The move took him by surprise and he pushed her back. Her lips were cold, devoid of any emotion. Her beauty was superficial. She used her body and her charms as a tool to get what she wanted from men, nothing more.

'Take me with you, you can protect me,' she said. 'I'll give you anything.' She wiggled out of the top of her robe, revealing herself completely to him, offering herself without compunction.

He uttered a lifeless laugh and turned away. 'You got nothing I want, ma'am.'

He turned and headed out of the room. 'You take my words serious,' he said over his shoulder to Brett. As he paused in the drawing-room entryway, he glanced back at the heavyset man, who was propped up on his elbows now. 'While you're at it, you might want to pray for forgiveness . . .'

Brett's face remained defiant. 'Get the hell out of my house, Travers.'

Calin frowned, shook his head, then headed for the front door, knowing men like Jared Brett rarely learned until it was too late.

Joe Sunkiller sat atop a palomino at the edge of the Brett property, watching Calin Travers ride off. A thin smile came to his lips. Had Travers figured it out so soon? Gone to warn Brett? He had to give the manhunter credit; he was a lot goddamn smarter than the others. None of them would have put the pieces together so fast. Perhaps he had made it too easy for him, but it didn't matter. Travers wouldn't be able to stop what was going to happen.

The front door opened and he saw Jared Brett step out on to the porch. Brett stared off at the departing Travers and even from this distance Sunkiller could see the look of fury on the man's face. He was a leader no more. Travers had shown him that truth and for that Sunkiller supposed he owed the manhunter a measure of thanks. A blonde woman appeared behind Brett, pressed the side of her face to the door frame.

Sunkiller reached for the Winchester in his

saddleboot and pulled it free. He lifted it, steadying the sight on the man standing on the porch, then peered at his target for long minutes, finger feather-light on the trigger.

He uttered a soft laugh, lowered the rifle, then hurled it to the ground.

'Not personal enough, Brett. You won't get out of it that easy . . .'

He reined around, for the time being leaving Jared Brett to think about what Calin Travers had told him.

CHAPTER SIX

Fifteen years ago . . .

'You can't do this, Jared!' Calin yelled, grabbing the larger boy's arm. 'It don't matter she's an Injun, it ain't right.'

Six boys had gathered in the clearing beside Blood Creek, Calin Travers, Jared Brett, Jim Foster and three others. They were full of hell, all sons of wealthy folk in Sundown, except for Calin himself. Calin's folks were of modest means but he'd gotten into the gang on Jim Foster's recommendation. Now he realized it had been a mistake, one his gut told him he was forever going to regret. Calin knew Jared Brett intended to cross the line the moment he told them they were going to corner the Ute girl at the creek. Calin and Foster had tried to talk him out of the plan, but Brett had insisted upon it and now it was too late. Too late to help the girl and too late to discover the things you thought you wanted, being accepted by boys hell-bent on trouble, weren't worth anything at all.

The others, gathered in a circle, all looked at Calin as if he were plumb out of his mind, all except for Jim Foster, whose eyes held worry. Foster didn't want this either, but he was too afraid to speak up now that it had gone this far.

Sitting in the circle, back arched, fingers gouging into the ground, was a Ute girl of sixteen, a girl who'd thought it clever to flirt with the white boys in town, but who hadn't suspected just what devilry those boys were capable of, especially Jared Brett. She looked like a frightened doe. Tears streamed down her face and her eyes held terror. Brett had made them hide in the bushes to grab her when she'd come to the creek. He'd watched her for days, learned her routine, oddly obsessed with the girl. To her it had been a playful game, making eyes at Brett and the rest, giggling when they looked her way. But to Brett it had become a dark fantasy, one he'd talked about constantly. And the others followed his lead, simply because they were afraid not to. Including Calin himself.

She wasn't much younger than himself, Calin thought. So pretty yet so innocent. He'd turned seventeen a week ago and the rest were of the same age. Her buckskin dress was soiled and torn in places. A small beaded doll hung on a rawhide string about her neck. Bruises and scrapes showed on her face. Jared had been unnecessarily rough on her when she'd panicked and tried to get away.

He'd thrown her to the ground, kicked her in the side.

Jared Brett jerked his arm away from Calin and turned on him. 'What the hell's wrong with you, Travers? You ain't gone yellow on us, have you? This girl's a dumb Injun whore. You seen how she kept teasin' us.'

'She was just funnin', Jared,' Calin said, desperation invading his voice. 'She didn't mean for nothin' like this to happen. She's scared. Look at her.'

Jared grinned, cruel delight dancing in his eyes. 'I been lookin' at her. She's right pretty for a squaw and she's gonna learn it ain't polite to tease a fella and not go through with it. You got no belly for it, you run on home to your ma and pa.'

'Jared, please, think about what you're doin'.' Calin struggled to keep his voice steady. He knew he was playing with fire. Jared scared him; the boy scared everyone in town his age.

Jared gave Calin a hard shove. 'Goddamn, if you ain't a yellow Nancy. Probably don't even like girls, do ya? We should have never let you come along with us. You ain't our kind, anyway, Travers. You're too poor and too yellow. Takes balls to ride with the Brett Gang.'

The Brett Gang. That's what Jared liked to call this bunch, as if they were outlaws on the owlhoot. But they weren't and Calin realized that now. They were simply trouble, irresponsible ruffians. And things were about to go beyond that.

Calin's gaze went to the girl, who was looking up at him with desperation in her tear-filled eyes. She didn't even speak English but he knew she understood he was trying to help her.

'What about the rest of you?' Calin asked, hoping against odds he could get at least Foster on his side.

The other boys chuckled. One of them spat at him. Jim Foster looked at the ground, unable to meet Calin's gaze. They wouldn't go against Jared, that was plain. Better to ride with the Devil than to chance his wrath.

Jared gave Calin another shove. Calin felt his legs get syrupy, fear running through his veins like poison.

'Go home, Travers. You ain't wanted in the Brett Gang no more.'

Jared turned back to look at the girl, who uttered a small sound of fright. He began to unhitch his belt buckle.

Calin didn't know what gave him the courage to try one more time. He'd never felt so consumed with fear and he knew that if the other boy decided to turn on him he had no chance to win in a fight.

'Jared, I'll tell the marshal. I'll tell somebody to come out here if you don't let her go.'

It was the wrong thing to say and he knew it the moment Jared's head swung and he saw fury redden the other boy's face. His fear got the better of him, then. He whirled, tried to run.

He didn't make it two steps before the larger boy grabbed him. Jared spun him around, hurled him to the ground.

Brett stood over him, hand balled into a tight fist. 'You yellow little sonofabitch. Don't you know Injuns ain't real people? They're killers, pure and simple, and here you are trying to protect one of them. What kind of white man are you, Calin? Don't you know we's fightin' with their kind?'

'There's . . . there's a treaty comin', Jared. And that girl's never done nothin' to any of us.'

Jared laughed then kicked Calin in the mouth. Calin's teeth crashed together and agony splintered through his jaw. He uttered a pained sound and fell back on to his side, hand going to his mouth, blood streaming from his lips and tears flooding his eyes. Don't cry, he pleaded with himself. Please, don't cry. Anything but that.

One of the boys yelled, 'Give 'im a lickin', Jared.' Jim Foster turned his back, unable to watch.

Calin tried to get to his feet and scramble away, but Jared grabbed him and hauled him up.

'You peckerwood, you shoulda just kept your mouth shut and had some fun. Now I gotta shut it for you.' Jared let Calin go and Calin felt frozen where he stood. The heavier boy smashed him full in the face and an explosion of pain radiated through Calin's teeth.

Calin's legs threatened to go in different directions. In self-preservation he tried to swing a fist, but the move was awkward and didn't come close to connecting with the larger boy.

Jared swept a foot out that slammed against

Calin's left calf. Calin's leg went out from under him and he hit the ground hard on his back.

Jared Brett jumped atop him, pounding at his face with a fist. Each blow hit just hard enough to hurt like hell but not end consciousness. Jared was an expert at prolonging agony. Calin had seen him do it before, sometimes torturing small animals or old horses. Brett liked to see things suffer and Calin Travers would be no exception.

The beating didn't take long, but to Calin it felt like an eternity. When it was over he had lost at least one tooth and his nose was broken, streaming blood. He lay groaning in the sand, Brett standing over him, laughing that mocking laugh of his, a glee on his face that only came when he was having fun at another's expense.

'You should have just kept quiet, you sorry bastard,' Brett said. 'Get the hell out of here, Travers. You say a goddamn word to anyone and I'll make sure next time you ain't able to walk away. You know no one in this town can do nothin' anyway. My parents got too much money.'

Jared Brett ended his words by spitting on Calin and giving him a final kick in the side.

Then he turned away and went to the other boys. Calin lay there groaning, but not for long. Because a moment later he couldn't bear the sounds of the Indian girl's frantic cries.

He struggled to his feet, every inch of his body screaming with pain. He suspected maybe a bone of two might be fractured, but it didn't stop him from running like a scared rabbit. He dove on to the trail that led from the creek, stumbling, righting himself, running as hard as he was capable, given his condition. He didn't stop until he could no longer hear the girl's pitiful pleas or the sound of her clothes ripping.

Calin Travers came from his memory with a shudder and a surge of guilt. He stared for long moments at the bubbling creek before him, its reddish waters a mute reminder of what had occurred on its bank fifteen years previously. He recollected reaching town and telling his parents he had been thrown from a wild horse he'd tried to ride. They hadn't believed him but he had never told them the truth.

He had been a coward and what happened to that Indian girl after those boys had done their deed was still a mystery to him. He had never dared ask, even Jim Foster, whose face carried a peculiar reflection of guilt whenever Calin and he crossed paths. He could not blame Foster, because they were both the same. Frightened boys, guilt-ridden men.

'Christ . . .' he mumbled, gritting his teeth, giving a rock at his foot an angry kick. How could he have let all these years pass without confronting Brett and the others? He should have come back before now, tried to do something, anything, though he was damned if he knew what he could have done. He could never have proved anything against any of them. Those boys had been protected by their parents' wealth and no one would have given a damn what happened to an Indian girl. No one but Calin Travers and an unknown killer.

That girl. What had become of her? If he found her today would it matter? Could he say he was sorry, promise her he would find a way to bring Jared Brett to justice for what he had done to her when no white man's court would take her word or his against that of a man as rich as Jared Brett?

It might prove an empty promise and he was not the type of manhunter who doled out justice on his own. He brought men in to face charges, killed them when they forced him into it, but he did not set himself up as an executioner, nor could he let the killer stalking those who used to belong to the Brett Gang take vengeance on Jared Brett.

Either way he saw it as no win.

'Sonofabitch,' he muttered, wishing for once he could ignore duty and conviction and just let the cards fall where they might.

'You got any background information on this Joe Sunkiller?' asked Calin.

Tompkins looked up as Calin approached his desk. He shrugged. 'Not a hell of a lot. Like I said, came in almost a year back. Spends most of his time at the saloon, hasn't caused any trouble I'm aware of.'

Calin doffed his hat and glanced at the cell holding Jim Foster. The man still sat hunched on the cot, swaying, legs drawn up to his chest. He was quiet for the moment.

Calin seated himself in the hardbacked chair in front of the desk.

'Anyone one associate with him other than the woman who runs the general store?'

'Might check with Old Sam. He's the last of the Utes left in town. If Sunkiller was part of the same band he'd know it.'

'Where would I find this Old Sam?'

Tompkins sighed. 'He's a sad case. Wanders around the burned-out ruins of his village outside of town, south side. You'll either find him there or at Skeeter's Lodge, playing checkers with some of the old fellas.'

Calin nodded at Foster. 'He said anything?'

'Stopped babbling about two hours ago and hasn't made a sound since.'

'Annette Pickler, you know much about her?'

Tompkins shrugged. 'Husband was killed in a robbery. She took over the store. Nice enough lady, keeps to herself. Owns a small cabin and pays her mortgage on time.'

'Ever notice the bruises on her face?'

Tompkins eyes narrowed. 'What are you gettin' at, Calin? I know that look in your eye. And as I recollect when you start askin' things that don't seem related you're seein' connections others don't.'

Calin leaned forward, putting his elbows on the desk. 'Not sure I know myself, Hank. Pickler and Sunkiller are gettin' hitched this summer, but I got the impression she's not jumpin' out of the saddle over it. Look on her face when he came in the store made me think she was scared of him. Got a notion from the bruise on her cheek he's hittin' her, though she wouldn't admit to such.'

Tompkins let out a long sigh. 'Can't do much about it, then, 'less I see him do it or she's of a mind to report him.'

'How many women are gonna do that, Hank? Nothin' likely be done about it in most towns and she probably figures he'll just beat her worse if she says somethin'.' Calin couldn't keep the bitterness out of his tone and Tompkins caught it, eyed him seriously.

'There's something you ain't sayin', Calin. Got a notion it might relate to that ghost you used to ride with. Comin' back here cause that ghost to saddle up again?'

Calin gave a reluctant nod. 'More somethin' about this case, I figure.' Calin's eyes went distant. 'Somethin' happened . . . a long time ago. Couldn't do nothing about it then, but now . . . don't want the Pickler woman to make a mistake that's going to haunt her for the rest of her days. I got a notion those days won't be long, either, she marries a man like Sunkiller.'

'What happened? Did it involve these men whose wives were killed?'

'Reckon. Too many things point to it, and I ain't a man who cottons to coincidence.'

'And Sunkiller, you got a notion he's part of it, too?'

'Can't see how as of yet, but, yeah, I got him pegged for something. I can't prove it, but was hopin' I could get Pickler to point the way.'

'You'll need to gain her trust, if what you say about Sunkiller hittin' her is true.'

Calin nodded. 'Not going to be easy. Sometimes folks get so used to a situation . . . they can't see there's better. Whatever the case, I got a notion Jared Brett's wife will be next on our killer's list, and soon if I don't stop him.'

Tompkins paused, studied Calin a long moment. 'What about you, Calin? You on that list somehow?'

Calin stood, offering Tompkins a grim smile. 'I ain't married, Hank. What do I have to lose?'

Hank Tompkins shook his head. 'I reckon that's sidesteppin' the question, Calin.'

Calin uttered an easy laugh and left the office.

Joe Sunkiller stepped from around the corner of the marshal's office, leading his palomino by the reins. He watched Calin Travers ride for the end of town, confident of where the man was headed. Travers was putting the pieces together quickly, now. He remembered Blood Creek.

Sunkiller looked down at the object clutched tightly in his left hand, a bow he'd fashioned from dogwood months back when at first he'd considered simply slaughtering all the white men responsible for Blood Creek. He'd given up that notion quickly; it would be too easy a fate for such soulless men. They had to suffer, feel the pain Crying Dove had felt, the pain *he* had felt. They had to lose what mattered most to them, their loved ones, their precious white man's possessions.

Travers was different. He had no woman in his life, little in the way of belongings. So the bow would be a warning to him, a portent that his time was coming soon and when that time came Joe Sunkiller would cut off his hands and feet and leave him a quivering husk who wished he had been granted a merciful death.

But that would wait until after Jared Brett answered for his crime.

Calin slowed his horse to an easy walk as he approached the burned-out ruins of the Ute village. His gaze narrowed. The camp, nestled on three sides by forest which had encroached over the years of neglect, was barely more than strewn pieces of charred wood and singed bison skins from what had once been lodges. He noted a scattering of belongings – pieces of blankets, deteriorating quivers, a chipped doll head – some partly buried, others such as old utensils and pans rusted or broken.

A somber sight, the camp was a decrepit memory of a time fifteen years past, empty, forgotten by most. The derelict village seemed pervaded by a haunted feeling, the whispers of ghosts drifting on the breeze, glimpses of proud warriors vanishing into the past. Calin wondered whether that Indian girl had come back to this village after Blood Creek. Had she told her people what had happened to her? Had they ignored her, treated her as a pariah? Calin recalled never seeing her in town again after that day. After the treaty most Ute had left these parts, headed to a reservation. Had she gone with them? Had she hidden in shame amongst her people? Worse?

He wondered if Old Sam could answer those questions, but he saw no sign of the Ute in the camp.

He reined up, dismounted and walked a few yards into the ruins. A breeze stirred shreds of hide lying about, moaned through old wood.

Ghosts. There were plenty of those to go around, weren't there? For the red and the white man alike. The things men did to each other, to those different from themselves. Atrocities had been committed by both sides.

The Utes had been called savages. Calin had to wonder if that wasn't what all men came down to. What he had seen in his years as a manhunter, what those boys had done to that girl that day . . . how did that make man any better than beasts?

Some men were good, he reminded himself. He had to hope they outnumbered and out-gunned the bad. He had to hope that somehow in the end justice won out and those responsible for hurting others got their just reward.

Behind him, his chestnut shifted feet, nickered softly. The horse had caught a scent or heard a slight sound from the forest. Calin's manhunter's sixth sense made his gut cinch. He felt it, too. Eyes, watching him.

Making no sudden motion that might alert a stalker that he'd been discovered, Calin, in a natural movement, eased up the brim of his hat and scanned the surrounding woods.

Whoever dogged him was good. He spotted nothing but the sound of a small animal scurrying somewhere told him the watcher had shifted position. He was tempted to draw his Peacemaker, but that might only provoke an attack and he was out in the open, an easy target. His gaze swept sideways, seeking possible shelter. He saw a boulder fifteen feet to his left.

A *shrickkk* sound came, so sudden and so quick he got no time to react. Something blazed out of the forest straight towards him.

Pain lanced across his shoulder as the material of his shirt split and a streak of blood appeared in the flesh beneath.

'Christ!' he muttered, diving for the boulder and getting behind it. He gazed at the wound on his shoulder; it was superficial but it hurt like hell. His attention traveled back to where he'd been standing, traced the path of whatever had cut him backward from that point. An arrow was lodged into a charred board sticking out of the ground.

His gaze swept back in the direction from which the arrow had been fired. The sudden sounds of someone retreating hastily through the brush, abandoning stealth, reached his ears.

Calin's hand whisked for his Peacemaker as he jumped from behind the boulder and ran towards the woods. He plunged into the forest, using less caution than he should have, but he was reasonably sure that whoever had fired the arrow shot was now intent only upon escape.

It occurred to Calin that the attacker could have easily put that arrow into his heart, but hadn't. Why?

Because it was a warning, Calin. A warning you're getting close and that soon your own time will come.

Branches slapped at his face and snagged his trousers as he ran. He leaped over deadfalls and avoided jutting pieces of fallen branches. Pausing, he listened. The attacker had gone silent and he got no bearing on the bowman's direction.

A bird squawked. The breeze rustled leaves. His own heart thundered in his throat and his pulse throbbed in his ears. His green eyes roved and his gun followed their motion. He saw nothing, heard nothing, and it became apparent to him the attacker had made noise on purpose, as a challenge for him to follow. It was a sick game and whoever was behind the attack wanted Calin to know it was one he couldn't win. Calin waited another fifteen minutes, then gave it up. The bushwhacker was gone, as if he'd been nothing more than one of the ghosts haunting the Ute camp.

He holstered his gun and returned to his horse, glancing a last time at the woods before mounting.

An arrow. That made it obvious, didn't it? He doubted Old Sam would be firing off at strangers, so that left Joe Sunkiller. And Calin reckoned

Sunkiller knew full well Calin would pin him instantly as the man behind the bow. He also knew that without a shred of proof there was goddamn nothing Calin could do about it.

He's throwing down the gauntlet, Calin. He's practically admitting he's behind the killings . . .

Calin sighed, frustration trickling into his veins. He wasn't used to being a step behind the men he went after and he could not afford that if he intended to save the lives of a little girl, Sally Ann Brett, Annette Pickler and himself.

Skeeter's Lodge smelled of sweat and old urine. Small tables and numerous hardbacked chairs, sofas with torn leather and stuffing poking through filled the main room. A pot-bellied stove squatted near the south wall. The lodge itself was constructed of log, with thick support posts spaced evenly about the room. Hewn beams criss-crossed the ceiling.

Calin, stepping into the cabin a half-hour after the attack at the ruins – he'd stopped briefly at the doc's to tend to his shoulder wound and change shirts – scanned the handful of old men, some sleeping on the sofas, others hunched over tables, heads hanging. The sight made his heart cinch; it reminded him of the empty Ute village, desolate and forgotten, men fading into twilight alone, hardly living.

His attention settled on one man in a back corner, sitting at the table with a checker board before him. The man looked older than anyone Calin could recollect ever having seen. His wispy gray hair hung to his sharp shoulders and more wrinkles lined his weathered face than an old saddle. Fringed buckskins hung loosely on his skeletal frame and looked nearly as old as the man wearing them.

Calin walked over to him and the man looked up, his yellowed eyes reflecting a certain sense of haunting sadness.

'Do you play checkers?' the old man asked, his voice like twigs scratching over stone.

Calin nodded. 'Been known to.'

'Sit,' the man said. 'Please.'

Calin pulled out a chair and tossed his hat on to the table. He lined up the black pips on his side of the board.

'You are Old Sam?' he said, watching the Indian line up the checkers on his own side.

'Yes.' The Ute didn't lift his head. He studied the board. 'You wish to ask me something?'

Calin nodded. 'There's a man in town, name of Joe Sunkiller. You know of him?'

The old man's head lifted, a small fire sparking in his eyes.

'Do not befriend this man.'

Calin shook his head. 'Wasn't my intention to. Fact, I reckon he might have been downright unfriendly to me a short spell ago.'

'He was never right in the head . . .' Old Sam moved a checker.

'How so?'

Old Sam cleared his throat, frowned. 'He was a member of our band, many years ago. Then he went away.'

Calin's brow knotted. 'Went away?'

Old Sam nodded, gaze remaining on the board. 'He was taken to a white man's asylum. He did not return for many years.'

'He's back.'

'But he is the same, perhaps worse.'

'How do you know?'

Old Sam looked up, eyes weary. 'There is nothing but hate living in his eyes now. When a man has nothing but hate he is no longer a man at all.'

'Not sure I get your meanin'.' Calin jumped one of Old Sam's men, placed the captured checker to the side of the board.

'Many times before the treaty I watched Joe Sunkiller, from the time he was a boy until he became a young brave. He fought with the other boys in our band. In a fit of anger, he killed one of them over a child's game. Then he met Crying Dove and she quelled some of the rage that dwelled within him.'

'This Crying Dove, she's no longer with him?'

Old Sam's gaze locked with Calin's and Calin saw deep sorrow bleed from within the old man's weary brown eyes.

'She . . . left . . .' Old Sam's voice quivered. Calin got the notion there was something he wasn't saying.

'And Sunkiller?'

'His rage became like the starving panther. His mind . . .' Old Sam paused, as if struggling to find words. 'The white men took him away.'

Calin nodded, sensing more to the story and that the old man was either unwilling or unable to go further with it.

They finished the game in silence and Old Sam, for all his years, was still sharp enough to beat a man nearly a third his age at checkers in a handful of moves.

Calin stood, placed his hat on his head. 'There was a young Indian girl about fifteen years back . . . she . . . something might have happened to her near the creek. You know of her?'

Bleakness washed into old man's eyes. A moment dragged by. 'I do not know this girl of whom you speak . . .' he mumbled at last, then went back to stacking checkers.

Calin nodded, then headed for the door. The old man was plainly lying, but he doubted he'd be able to pry his secrets from him.

It was almost sundown when Old Sam approached the ruins of his village. His mind had become troubled by the things the young man had asked him at the lodge, and weary because he had chosen to hide the truth about Crying Dove and Joe Sunkiller. But it was so long ago and those days had vanished with the memories of the mighty band the Ute once were.

The Grandfather Above had turned His face from the Ute but He had cursed Joe Sunkiller many many moons ago. Violence and bloodshed had never ceased to follow the boy, from the moment of his birth until the day the white man took him away. Now it was worse. Perhaps he should have told the white man everything; perhaps the white man could stop Joe Sunkiller before more blood ran cold into the ground.

Old Sam sighed a weary sigh, eyes tearing up as he gazed at the ruins. He was tired, so very tired.

Why should he tell the white man anything? Why should he bother saving any of their people? He had signed the treaty with them and now they had everything, his people's land, his people's pride.

All that remained for him was his checkers, when someone would play with him, and the old spirits that haunted his dreams and the remains of this camp.

A laugh came from behind him and he turned. A man stood there, battered hat pulled low, black duster jostled by the breeze. A Bowie knife glinted in his hand.

'What did you tell Travers, old man?' came the figure's voice.

'Joe Sunkiller . . .' Old Sam muttered, his old heart beating a step faster.

'You remember me . . .'

'How could I forget the One Whom Darkness Stalks? You don't belong to this village anymore. The Grandfather Above shunned you.'

Joe Sunkiller took a step closer, coming only a handful of inches from the old man. 'Foolishness. Foolish Indian ways. Look around you, there's nothing here but the white man's empty promises. You signed their worthless treaty. You consigned your band to extinction.'

Old Sam's lips quivered and emotion lodged in his throat. 'I did what I had to do to stop the slaughter. We all would have died.'

'We all *did* die, you short-sighted old bastard. If you would have let me make those boys pay that day . . .'

'The white man would have come and killed us all, men, women, children. I could not let that happen.'

'Yet you let the crimes against Crying Dove go unpunished.'

'*They* did not kill her . . .'

Joe Sunkiller scoffed. 'They surely did. What they did to her . . . she could not have lived with the shame . . .'

'That choice should have been hers.'

Joe Sunkiller smiled a coyote smile. 'Sometimes choices are made for us . . .' He jerked up the knife and buried it in Old Sam's belly. The old man looked down to see the hilt sticking out of his stomach, then back to Sunkiller. Blood dribbled from the corner of his mouth. He struggled to say something but pain swallowed his words and great black wings fluttered from the corners of his mind.

CHAPTER SEVEN

Morning came in a blaze of brassy sunlight and soft spring air. Water troughs sparkled with gems of amber and the sweet scent of fresh pine drifted in from the surrounding forest. The day appeared utterly serene, one like any other, but Calin saw the darkness beneath its surface. A killer stalked the town and old memories of a long ago day dogged his soul.

Along with those memories came a measure of growing frustration. As he headed for the café, his thoughts struggled with the notion that Joe Sunkiller was likely a murderer yet he had no way of proving it, stopping him. Either somebody, Annette Pickler or Old Sam, had to talk – and neither seemed inclined – or he had to catch the Ute in the act. The problem with the latter was that the lives of a little girl and Sally Ann Brett were at stake and any misstep might get them killed.

At the café he downed a quick breakfast of bacon, eggs and half a pot of Arbuckle's, then headed back along the boardwalk. Where was Sunkiller this morning? Stalking Brett's wife? With Annette Pickler? Calin passed the saloon, took a quick look through the window, getting the answer to his question. Sunkiller sat at a table, eating breakfast. Good, that would occupy the man for a short spell.

Calin had settled on another option, one he hinged little hope on but reckoned it was worth a try. He'd gotten the address for Sunkiller's shack from Tompkins after reporting the arrow incident to him late yesterday. Tompkins had promised to talk with Brett, try to get him to put his wife in protective custody, but he was of the mind that Jared would refuse any help from the law. Calin had to agree. They couldn't force protection on Mrs Brett against Jared's will and unless she placed herself in custody they were at an impasse. Calin knew Brett would never allow her to accept help. He was too arrogant and likely still carried the notion no one would dare strike at a Brett. Calin hoped Brett didn't learn his lesson the hard way, for his wife's sake.

Calin edged away from the window, headed along the boardwalk. While he doubted he'd find much of consequence at Sunkiller's cabin, if he at least found a bow or other arrows it might be enough to have Tompkins bring in the Ute for a day or two and buy him some much needed time. He wagered the Indian wouldn't wait long before striking at Jared Brett and even a day might mean the difference in preventing more death.

Although he was convinced Sunkiller was his man, he still found himself sifting through questions, searching for missing pieces. What connection did the man have to that day fifteen years ago, to the Indian girl? How did he know who was responsible for what had happened to her? Had she told him? Had she mentioned Calin Travers to him as well?

Who was that girl? Was she the one Old Sam mentioned, Crying Dove? Where had she gone? The more he thought over the old man's words the more he didn't like the way Old Sam's tone had darkened when he mentioned the girl. It gave Calin a cold feeling in his belly, one that told him locating the girl now was out of the question.

A woman stepped on to the boardwalk ahead of him, and the sight of her drew him from his thoughts. She went to the door of the general store, inserted a key into the lock. As if she knew he was watching, her head turned towards him, momentary surprise jumping on to her face, perhaps even a hint of pleasure. It quickly dissolved into worry as he came up to her.

'Miss Pickler . . .' His voice trailed off as he studied her face, his belly sinking as he focused on the fresh bruise and cut on her cheek. She quickly turned away, realizing what he was looking at.

'Mr . . . Mr Travers . . .' Her voice came shaky, hesitant. She tried to turn the handle and get inside, but he gently took her elbow, stopping her.

'Sunkiller did that to you, didn't he? You can tell

108

me, ma'am. I can protect you from him.'

She looked at him, confusion and a specter of skepticism on her features. 'Like those other women got protection from that killer . . .'

'What're you sayin', Miss Pickler?'

She shook her head. 'Nothing. I'm saying nothing.'

She was lying and he knew it. His gaze held hers and he saw an inner beauty show through that countered the lies coming out of her mouth. He felt convinced she wasn't hiding things out of malice. She was afraid, deathly afraid, and he couldn't rightly blame her.

'Did Joe Sunkiller hit you, Miss Pickler?' he asked again, voice steady, gently demanding.

'I . . . I was trying to fix a shutter on my home and it fell off and hit me in the face. I'll be fine.'

Again the lie was plain in her voice. He frowned. 'I wish you'd trust me enough to tell me what really happened, Miss Pickler. I'm trying to stop these killings. If Joe Sunkiller's responsible, I need to know, because it won't be long before he kills you, too, either by design or by accident.'

She peered at him, searching his eyes and for one of the few times in his life he felt something he'd never experienced before, the notion that if given time he might become attached to her, perhaps feel something even stronger.

She reached up suddenly, her trembling fingers gently touching his cheek.

'You're a kind man, Mr Travers. A good man. I

can see it in your eyes. I know you mean what you say, but you can't be everywhere at every minute. It will be in one of those minutes that the worst happens. Please, please leave this town before . . . I don't want anything to happen to you, Mr Travers.'

He gave her a soft smile, his own hand drifting up and touching hers as it lay against his cheek. For a moment he didn't speak, then she pulled her hand away, a guilty expression crossing her eyes.

'I can't leave, Miss Pickler. There's a man sitting in the marshal's jail whose wits are gone, maybe permanently. And somewhere out there there might be a little girl who's terrified and doesn't understand the loss of her ma and pa. I need to stop these killings and find that child if she's still alive. And I need to see justice done.'

Annette Pickler looked down at the boardwalk for a long moment, as if thinking something over, but when her head lifted he saw tears welling in her eyes.

'I don't know anything, Mr Travers. I'm sorry. I'm just a weak woman tryin' to make ends meet and live to see another day. I'm not even sure why I care about goin' on, but I do.'

He nodded, again positive she was lying. 'You change your mind I'm at the Black Horse Hotel, Room 12. I meant what I said when I told you I would protect you.'

She nodded, then turned towards the door. 'Good day, Mr Travers.'

He tipped a finger to his hat brim and watched

her step inside, close the door.

Annette Pickler leaned back against the wall after she watched Calin Travers walk down the boardwalk. She let out a shuddering breath and forced back the tears flooding her eyes. She had come so close to telling him, trusting him, but how could she? How could she trust a man she had just met, a stranger?

Something in his eyes, she told herself. A deep kindness, a man who was haunted but trying to make up for some past sin. A man fighting the impossible. A man she might grow to love given a chance.

Travers was right. Joe Sunkiller was going to kill her. Maybe not today, maybe not tomorrow, but he would do it. His beatings were getting worse, his anger more unreined, and that would only escalate once they married.

And the little girl. . . .

A tear slipped from her eye. She couldn't keep this up. Because if Joe Sunkiller didn't beat her to death first, the secrets, the lies, would kill her just as surely.

Joe Sunkiller's cabin wasn't much to speak of. Calin surveyed the exterior of the ramshackle place on Jasper Street, noting dangling shutters and debris scattered about its sparse grounds. A window was broken, boarded over. The roof looked ready to cave in. Calin got the notion that that made it even more likely the man wasn't about to leave evidence lying around inside, nor would he hide a little girl there, either.

Calin tried the front door, finding it open, which he reckoned confirmed his theory. He slipped into the cabin and eased the door shut behind him. The place consisted of one large room with meager furnishings – a sheetless cot in one corner, a hard-backed chair with a blanket draped over its back and a small rolltop desk, nothing else. Not even a skillet or pan, drinking glass or pillow. Dust and grime lay heavy on the floorboards. He saw no sign of a bow, quiver or arrows. Had he been a betting man he would have wagered Sunkiller'd stashed the weapon somewhere in the woods.

Calin stepped deeper into the room, gripped by a sense of emptiness. He saw no personal effects, nothing to indicate a man had lived instead of merely existed here for the past year. No tintypes of Annette Pickler, a woman he intended to marry, no sign of gifts she might have given him. Maybe that was the type of man it took to butcher innocent women, Calin thought. A man with no attachments, no sentimentalities. A man as empty inside as this room.

He suppressed a shudder at the thought. Calin reckoned he had no desire to dwell too long on the type of man capable of committing such evils, only the burning need to stop him.

He went to the rolltop desk, figuring that if Sunkiller had anything personal he would stow it there. Upon lifting the front he discovered the pigeon holes to be empty. With a sigh, he lowered the top, then began pulling out the drawers. The first two were empty but the third held a small beaded trinket of some sort. Calin's eyes narrowed as he took the trinket from the drawer, examined it. It was a small Indian figure made of rawhide laced with multicolored beads.

His lips parted slightly and something tugged at his memory.

He'd seen it before, somewhere. . . .

Calin's belly cinched. He remembered, now. He'd seen it that day, fifteen year ago. Around that Indian girl's neck.

And Sunkiller had it now.

He replaced the trinket and slid the drawer shut. That confirmed a link from Sunkiller to that girl, to Calin's thinking. Sunkiller and he appeared to be roughly the same age, the Ute perhaps a year or two older. Could that girl have been the Crying Dove Old Sam spoke of? Calin was damn near certain of it, now. It made sense, provided the motivation for the Ute striking at the boys who had been at the creek that day. But why wait fifteen years? And why exact such brutal vengeance on women who'd had no part in the deed?

Because he's insane, Calin. He spent all those years in an asylum, planning for the moment he could make them suffer for what they had done, then more time stalking them, learning their every habit before making his move. That's what he's doing with Brett, now, learning his

113

routines, scouting his prey . . .

Calin frowned, backed from the room. He had nearly all the pieces now; only the details needed to be filled in. He reckoned his next step was to confront Joe Sunkiller with his suspicions and hope he could shake the man into making a mistake. Because without proof he wouldn't be able to prevent more deaths, including his own.

The past is forever. There is no present, no future, only what was. And what was haunts eternally.

Joe Sunkiller sat atop his palomino, gazing out at the bubbling waters of Blood Creek. The breeze stirred the strands of hair filtering from beneath his low-pulled hat. His horse snorted. A small animal scurried somewhere in the woods behind him. The past fell like a dark cloud across his bleeding soul.

Another ten minutes passed before he climbed from the palomino and tethered the horse to a branch. His dark eyes glittered with daggers of hate as he went to the water's edge and knelt in the soft sand. His lips drew into a hard line.

He had not come back to this place since returning to Sundown. But through all those years he'd been confined in the white man's institution he had thought about it, remembered the last day he'd stood on its bank. Remembered what those white boys had done to Crying Dove.

His years away had made him stronger. They'd educated him at the institution, taught him patience. But the sweet fire of vengeance burning

114

in his belly had never died.

Fifteen years ago his band had sacrificed Crying Dove in order to sign their precious treaty and save their own skins by refusing to let him make those boys answer for their crime. But his people were no longer here to stop him. No one could stop him. Not Sam Running Elk, whose body he had left to the buzzards, nor Calin Travers.

He laughed a chilled laugh and scooped a handful of sand from the bank. He watched it trickle through his fingers.

But it was no longer sand, was it? It was blood. Her blood.

He was suddenly atop a horse on the trail leading through the woods towards the creek, a blanket for a saddle, a young brave who had ridden from camp in search of the girl promised to him as a wife, the girl who spent too much time smiling and gazing upon a certain few white boys of Sundown. Crying Dove thought it a game, teasing those boys, but he knew better. He knew the white men and their ways, knew the fire she heedlessly fanned.

He stopped the pony, listening for any sign of her. He knew she had come this way; she did so each day at this time, to watch the red-brown water.

Sounds. Someone was coming, someone in a hurry.

He eased his horse back, getting behind a large clump of brush within the tangled trees that grew unbridled along the side of the trail.

He slipped off his mount, dark eyes narrowing.

115

The sounds grew louder and at last he saw the boy running along the trail. Blood flowed from the boy's nose and mouth and his face was battered. He half-stumbled, half-ran. Joe Sunkiller recognized him from town, one of the boys who'd befriended that bunch led by Jared Brett, the rich white man's son. Travers was his name.

The boy staggered past, and Joe Sunkiller could see he was crying, gasping. A simmering dread came to Joe Sunkiller's belly. Something had happened.

The boy went on, disappearing in the direction of town.

He eased his mount back on to the trail, climbed atop it, then headed towards the creek. After stopping a few hundred yards further on he dismounted and tethered the horse to a cottonwood branch, then made his way forward on foot.

By the time he reached Blood Creek it was too late. He saw five boys standing over Crying Dove, who lay on the ground, curled into a fetal position, nearly all her clothing torn off. Blood ran down her thighs and tears streamed down her face.

The boys were laughing, pointing at her, the Brett boy buckling his trousers. Each of their faces burned into his memory with pure hatred, unbridled fury.

Rage overcame him and he lost all sense of caution. He saw only red, wanted only to pound their faces to a gory pulp with his fists, then slice off their manhood with the knife at his waist and bind it in their mouths.

His bounded forward, hurling himself at the boys. Brett whirled, reacting with a mocking laugh and a sidestep. The larger boy hammered a blow to the side of Joe's head as he plunged past. The others made a grab for him.

The blow shook him but he managed to get in a couple punches to one of the others, before he went down beneath an avalanche of striking fists. They kicked at him, breaking ribs, shattering his nose. He heard Brett laughing and whooping.

'Goddamn stupid Injun!' Brett shouted, kicking him again. 'Your girl wasn't even worth the trouble. Shoulda known an Injun couldn't please no one but another Injun.'

It was over a few minutes later. They left him lying in the sand, groaning, bleeding, pain lancing every inch of his body. Lying there for what seemed like hours. The only sound that of Crying Dove's eternal sobbing.

The sun had begun to drift behind the trees in the west by the time he was able to push himself to his hands and knees. Blood streamed from his mouth into the sand. Hate, rage, vengeance rushed through his veins. He would find those boys, make each of them pay for what they had done to Crying Dove. But first he had a duty, one that brought him great sorrow but one that was necessary to preserve her honor, as well as his own.

He gazed at Crying Dove, who was still curled into a ball, weeping inconsolably. He gazed at her long and regretfully, darkness moving across his eyes. His hand drifted to the knife at his waist.

She was no longer pure, unworthy of him, unworthy of life. Those boys had soiled her and she would not be his bride when the summer sun rose high.

He crawled over to her and she looked at him, terror and pain in her soft brown eyes.

'I will free you from your shame,' he mumbled, voice shaking. She must have realized what he intended, for she began screaming. She screamed until his knife cut deep into her throat. He buried her when the moon rose, in a white man's grave in the woods.

As Joe Sunkiller came back to the present, his hand now empty of sand, a single tear flowed down his cheek. His band had not understood his noble sacrifice. They had branded him a dog barking at the moon. They'd refused his pleas to let him punish those boys, and they had looked upon him with disgust and shame.

Then they had sent him away. . . .

A sound broke his reverie and he turned to see a man sitting on a horse behind him.

Calin tried the saloon first in his search for Joe Sunkiller, but the Ute had left and the barkeep had no idea where he had gone. Next he glanced into the general store window but Sunkiller was not there, either. Upon running into Tompkins on the street, he learned the marshal had seen Sunkiller headed north about fifteen minutes ago, but was unaware of the Ute's destination.

Calin reckoned he had an idea where the Indian was headed. Blood Creek lay in the direction.

He saddled his chestnut and headed to the trail that led through the woods to the creek. If the Ute wasn't there Calin didn't really care to think about the alternative. Sunkiller might have decided to move on Brett's wife, but the mansion lay in another direction, so it was a calculated risk.

Calin reined up when he reached the trail, then dismounted. He surveyed the ground, noting fresh hoofprints in the soft earth. Someone had come this way not more than a few minutes ago and Calin reckoned his hunch had been right. Joe Sunkiller *was* headed to Blood Creek.

He mounted, gigged his horse into an easy gait. A few moments later he came upon the opening that led to the creek and noticed a palomino tethered to a branch to the left. He drew up, gaze skipping from the horse to the man kneeling in the sand at water's edge. He paused, watching the man for long moments. Sunkiller seemed lost in thought. The Ute's body tensed every so often, as if he were reliving some painful memory.

Calin shifted in the saddle and Sunkiller's head came up, then around. The Ute made no attempt to hide the dark fury bleeding from his eyes and coldness washed through Calin's soul.

'It's you, isn't it?' Calin's gaze locked with the Ute's. 'You're responsible for the killings.'

Joe Sunkiller's face gained a measure of control

and the Ute stood, then turned towards Calin, eyes narrowed, dark, probing.

'You cannot prove it . . .'

'I will, somehow.'

'By then it will be too late. You cannot save Brett's woman and you cannot save yourself.'

Calin's hand drifted to the Peacemaker at his hip and for the briefest of moments he considered ignoring his convictions, his honor. 'I could hang you here . . .'

Joe Sunkiller's laugh mocked him. 'No, you could not. You are not that type of man. You are the coward who ran from the creek that day. You are the coward who left Crying Dove to Brett and the others and never said a word to anyone about what happened to a poor red girl.'

Guilt crawled through Calin's belly. 'I tried to stop them.'

'But you did not. And you did not honor Crying Dove by bringing them to justice, as you do others who wrong your kind.'

'I was a boy. I had no way of bringing charges against those others. No one would have believed me and even if they had, Brett and the rest, their folks were powerful, rich. Nothing would have been done.'

'You were afraid of them. All those years you let them walk free, knowing what they had done.'

Calin sighed. 'Reckon you might be right in that. Reckon I've been blaming myself ever since. But I'll see to it Brett pays now for his part in what happened that day, somehow.'

Sunkiller uttered a chilled laugh. 'Brett will pay, but not by your hand.'

'Leave his wife be, Sunkiller. She had no part in what happened.'

'Crying Dove did not ask for what happened to her, either. Did they listen to her pleas?'

Calin's head dropped. He stared at the ground, the memory of the girl's pleas biting into his conscience. His head came up, gaze centering on the Ute. 'Who was she to you, Sunkiller? Who was Crying Dove? Tell me, please. I want to know her.'

A pained look filtered across the Ute's face for an instant. 'She was promised to me. We would have married with the summer.'

'Where is she now?'

'She . . . Her spirit is clean.'

Calin's belly cinched. Something in the way Sunkiller said it verified his notion that Crying Dove was dead and he felt heartache for a girl he had never really known and perhaps some for himself. She was gone and with her went any chance of ever telling her how sorry he was for that day. 'You saw me that day? Saw the rest?'

Sunkiller nodded. 'I came upon them. They did the same to me as they did you, only I did not run.'

'You came back to Sundown a year ago. Reckon it took time for you to locate them all, settle on your plan.'

'I'm a patient man. I waited fifteen years, I could wait a few months more to make certain things went according to my plan.'

'You're admitting murder to me.'

'It does not matter. Your word will not hang me and I will deny it to all others.'

He was right. It would be his word against Sunkiller's. He'd never be convicted on that alone.

'I got my limits, Sunkiller. No matter what code I live by, you harm a hair on Foster's child, I'll put a bullet in you without regret.'

Joe Sunkiller laughed and turned to face the water. 'Go back to town, Travers. Go back and wait for me to come for you . . .'

'Stay away from Sally Ann Brett. I won't tell you again. You'll find out the coward I was fifteen years ago died the day I left Sundown.'

Sunkiller didn't turn back to him, didn't say a word.

Calin reined around. Despite what he just told the Ute, he wondered if he weren't simply running again, by leaving Sunkiller free. Wondered if his convictions weren't simply another excuse to appease that streak of yellow he'd always told himself was at fault for the way things had played in his life. Wondered it might not get Sally Ann Brett, Foster's child and Annette Pickler killed.

CHAPTER EIGHT

Calin Travers sat at a rear table in the café, across from Marshal Hank Tompkins. Late-afternoon sunlight filtered through blue-curtained windows. The marshal was eating an early dinner, while Calin sipped at a cup of Arbuckle's and stared out through the window into the street, absently watching passers-by filter along the boardwalk.

His mind played over the events of the past day and a half and his confrontation with Joe Sunkiller at Blood Creek. He was now certain the Ute was his killer, but the notion that he had nothing tangible upon which to bring the man to justice rankled him. Lives were in danger, a little girl's if she were still alive, Sally Ann Brett's, Annette Pickler's . . . his own. And at the moment he couldn't do a damn thing about it.

'Stop beatin' yourself up over it, Calin,' Tompkins said, then shoved a bite of beefsteak into his mouth.

'Huh?' Calin shook from his thoughts, glanced

about the café, which was deserted except for him and the lawdog. He leaned back in his seat, ran a finger over his upper lip.

'Won't do no good, ridin' yourself. Question is, what do we do about it now that we've got a suspect?'

'Wish to hell I knew, Hank.'

Tompkins chewed another piece of steak and swallowed. 'You never had much trouble with indecision back when we rode together.'

'Things were more black and white back then. You tracked down an outlaw and either he went peaceably or he didn't. Joe Sunkiller . . . well, he's another animal. I know he's behind all this but I can't prove it, so I can't bring him in and my conscience won't let me simply put a bullet in him.'

Tompkins frowned. 'Nothin' much I can do at this point, either. I rode out to the Brett place earlier and approached him about putting his wife into protective custody but Jared Brett ain't a man to be reasoned with. I got the notion he wouldn't even rightly care a lick if Sunkiller did fillet his wife.'

'Brett never cared about anyone except himself, I reckon. She's a possession to him, nothing more, one he figures he can easily replace. She doesn't give much of a damn about him, either, but she believed me enough to be frightened.'

Tompkins shrugged. 'Still, I can't help her if she won't come in.'

'Brett would never let her. It would be a sign of

weakness to him.'

Tompkins uttered an uneasy laugh. 'Which might make him an accessory to murder if anything happens to her, the way I see it. Least that's what I aim to haul his sorry ass in on should worse come to worst.' Tompkins paused. 'I'll put a deputy on the Brett place, tell him to stay out of sight, but that's the most I can do.'

'Reckon that'd be a good start. Sunkiller will make a move on Brett soon, I figure, and once he discovers Brett don't give a damn about his wife, he'll go after Brett's possessions, his house, maybe his life. I got the notion Sunkiller's riding a very thin edge.'

'Annette Pickler, you reckon she's in danger?'

'From what I saw in Sunkiller's cabin, he's a man who ain't putting down roots. I reckon Pickler's satisfying a need for the moment and when his goal's met he won't have much use for her anymore. I doubt he ever really intended to marry her.'

'And you figure he's got her so plumb scared she won't go against him?'

Calin sighed. 'She's a good woman. I could see it in her eyes. But I don't know if I have enough time left to gain her trust. Still, I'm itching to try again . . .'

Hank Tompkins peered at his friend, stabbed a bite of beefsteak with his fork, paused it halfway between his plate and his mouth. A slight grin came to his lips.

'Well, I never thought I'd live to see the day!'

Calin's green eyes narrowed. He wondered if his cheeks reddened because it sure as hell felt suddenly hot in the café. 'What's that s'posed to mean?'

'You never were a man any good at hiding his feelings, Calin. Even if you ain't realized it yet, you're sweet on that gal.'

'She's with Sunkiller.' Calin answered too quickly and too defensively.

'A man you suspect to be a cold-blooded killer. Reckon there's not a lot of future in that kind of relationship, now, is there?'

Calin scoffed, but the sound held more than a little worry. 'Especially if he kills *her*...'

'Then I recommend you get to her before he does. Convince her we can keep he safe.'

Calin cocked an eyebrow, 'Can we?'

Tompkins set the fork holding a piece of steak on the plate, his face turning serious. 'We can try our damnedest.'

'Sunkiller's cunning and violent and he's killed four other women. Can I honestly promise her he won't kill her and live up to my word?'

Hank frowned. 'That's not what's worryin' you, is it? That ghost you got doggin' you is back.'

Calin leaned forward, rested both elbows on the table. 'Fifteen years ago there were six boys, teenagers a step away from being men. Brett was the leader and those other men whose wives got killed, they followed him around like chicks following a mother hen. I wanted to fit in with them, Hank, least I thought I did. I wanted to be accepted, be part of the Brett Gang. Thought they were basically harmless, just boys bein' boys.'

'Didn't work out that way, I take it?'

Calin shook his head. 'No, it didn't.' Calin told Tompkins the story of that day at Blood Creek, how the boys had raped a Ute girl named Crying Dove and how he had run like a coward after trying to stop them. 'I've been carrying it around ever since, feeling guilty, wonderin' about that poor girl. I let it happen, let Brett and the rest hurt her and never said a word about it.'

'Jesus, Calin, you can't blame yourself for that.'

Calin uttered a humorless laugh. 'I've been doing a damn fine job of it for the last fifteen years.'

Hank Tompkins sighed, took a sip of his coffee, then leaned back in his chair. 'You were a boy. You weren't a coward. You stood up to those others and they beat the hell out of you. You kept it up they might have killed you. Their folks were rich, they practically owned the town. Even if you had said something it wouldn't have made any difference.'

'Would have made a difference to me, Hank. Would have made a difference to the man I've tried to be these past years.'

'Inclined to disagree and say it *made* you the man you are, made you realize there's injustice in this godforsaken world that needs tendin' to and you're the man who might be able to make a difference. Whatever the case, you were still a boy and not capa-

127

ble of makin' a man's decisions. You did your best. A coward wouldn't have even tried to go against five other boys.'

'That ain't the way Sunkiller sees it. He blames me for running as much as he blames the others for raping Crying Dove.'

'Sunkiller was never right in the head, accordin' to what you told me Old Sam said, and it don't take a gypsy crystal-gazer to see that if he's responsible for these killings the years haven't improved that any.'

'Still, I let it go for years, Hank. I never said anything, never did anything about it.'

Hank nodded. 'Reckon you paid for that enough with your guilt. You came back to Sundown and you'll fix it now. You'll give that girl honor, wherever she is.'

'She's dead.'

The marshal's brow knotted. 'How do you know that?'

'Sunkiller. Didn't say it directly, but his meanin' was plain. I got a notion he killed her out of some twisted sense of honor.'

'Then he's worse than all those boys, Calin. No matter what he was thinkin' that girl suffered enough with what Brett and his bunch did to her, but if Sunkiller took her life because of it he's the one you need to bring to justice to give her memory peace.'

Calin nodded, standing and grabbing his hat from the table. 'Just how am I s'posed to do that before he kills again? And how the hell am I going to find Foster's little girl?'

Hank's eyes narrowed, serious. 'You'll find a way, Calin. You always did and you always will. Give yourself some credit for being the kind of man I know you are.'

Calin nodded a parting nod, and left Tompkins to finish his meal.

Once outside in the afternoon sunlight he paused, taking a deep breath. What Tompkins had said made sense: he was blaming a boy for the things even a man would have had trouble confronting. He had tried to stop Brett that day but had faced impossible odds.

Those odds were different now, and it was time to set things right, save an innocent child and two women before they perished at the hands of a maniac.

But even if he did stop Joe Sunkiller, Jared Brett might never pay for his crime. The rape had occurred fifteen years ago and no white man's court would convict him for it, even on Calin's word. Since he had run, had not witnessed the actual deed, he could not testify to it. And since that Ute girl was dead, she could not accuse Brett. He had no evidence, no case. Brett had enough money to hire all the fancy East coast, frock-coated lawyers he needed to make certain he'd walk.

'I'm sorry . . .' he whispered to an Indian girl he had never known. 'I'm sorry I let things come to this and I'm sorry I couldn't help you that day.'

He sighed, walked along the boardwalk until he came to the general store. He hesitated, finding himself suddenly a bit nervous. He'd wanted to dismiss what the marshal had said about his feelings for Annette Pickler, but wondered if maybe Tompkins had seen something before Calin even realized it. Although he'd met the woman only twice, something about her put butterflies in his belly. He had never felt anything like it before and he had to admit it was a mite uncomfortable.

But for the moment it didn't matter. Any thoughts of her in a womanly capacity were improper and useless until Sunkiller was brought to justice.

He drew a deep breath, then entered the store, closing the door behind him.

Annette looked up from behind the counter at the clink of the bell. The look that flashed across her face was a mixture of warmth and worry. He started down the aisle and she came out from behind the counter, meeting him half way.

'Please, Mr Travers, you shouldn't be here. I told you all I could.' Her voice trembled, as if she were having a harder time keeping her secrets. He could tell things had been preying on her mind, whittling away her composure.

'Miss Pickler . . . Annette . . .' He liked the sound of her name on his lips and for the briefest of moments he saw she liked it, too. He decided to put it to her straight, determine if his instincts about her were right. 'Joe Sunkiller is a murderer. He's

130

brutally murdered four women and an Indian girl and kidnapped a child who may or may not have been another of his victims. Sally Ann Brett will die soon if you don't tell me everything you know and then he'll come for you.'

'Me. . . ?' Her fingers went to a bruise on her cheek. 'You have to leave this town, Mr Travers. Before he hurts you.'

'Calin,' he said. 'My name's Calin. And I can take care of myself now. But you and Brett's wife . . .'

She folded her arms about herself, shuddering, turning her gaze from him. 'I'll tell Joe to leave. I won't marry him. I've been living a lonely life since my husband died. I reckon I can go on that way.'

Calin frowned, gently taking her arms, making her face him. 'You know it won't be that simple. He won't let you go and he never really planned to marry you. He *will* kill you, Annette.'

She peered at the floor, darkness moving across her face. She knew he was right but was trying to convince herself otherwise. She shook for a moment and he had the sudden urge to pull her into his arms. Before he could stop himself he drew her close and she did not resist. She seemed to melt into him and he reckoned he'd never felt anything so utterly satisfying.

She looked up at him, lips parted slightly, trembling, and lifted on to her toes. Her lips pressed to his, searching, soft and tasting of ripe peaches.

The bell clinked above the door and she jerked away, a gasp escaping her lips.

Calin turned, saw Joe Sunkiller standing in the doorway. The Ute peered at them, fury washing across his face.

'This how you plan to stop me, Travers?' Sunkiller stepped deeper into the store, coming up to him. 'By stealing my woman and turning her against me?'

Calin never got the chance to answer. A fist hit him in the face and he flew backwards into a shelf stacked with canned goods. The cans tumbled to the floor and he wobbled, nearly going down. Only by sheer will did he manage to stay on his feet.

A thought flashed through his mind. He had managed to go years without fighting another man, and yet he now counted three in as many days. It was starting to piss him off.

Shaking off the blow, he sprang forward, still unsteady. Joe Sunkiller flew at him at the same time.

Sunkiller snapped three quick jabs. Calin avoided all but one but that had little power in it. It was meant to keep him off balance, overwhelmed, so the Ute could lob an arcing right that would have ended the fight. It might have worked on a man who hadn't spent the past ten years honing his fighting skills.

Calin slipped under the man's blow and buried a right in Sunkiller's breadbasket. A burst of air came from the Ute's lungs. He stumbled back a couple of steps, stopped swinging.

Calin seized the advantage, pivoting on a heel and delivering a sidekick that connected with

Sunkiller's short rib.

The Ute uttered a groan, his upper body jerking forward a few inches. Calin stepped in, delivering two short jabs to the Indian's mouth that mashed his lips with a spray of blood.

Sunkiller grunted, charged, driven by sheer fury. He swung from the floor; the blow whisked by Calin's chin as the manhunter jerked his head sideways. His hat flew from his head.

Calin countered with a sharp right straight down the pike. It hit the Ute flush on the nose but barely made him stutter in his step. Fury was overriding pain. Sunkiller launched a roundhouse.

Calin ducked under the blow, bobbed up, slammed a bootheel into the Ute's shin. Sunkiller's leg buckled slightly, but he held his feet. Calin hit him again in jaw.

For a moment Calin thought it was over. Sunkiller wavered, appeared ready to go down. The manhunter set himself to deliver a knockout blow.

Sunkiller was faking, at least partly, because the moment Calin cocked his arm the Indian fired back. Sunkiller suddenly stopped swinging with fury and started fighting with skill. He was hurt, unsteady, but still powerful.

He delivered a short uppercut that connected with a loud crack and slammed Calin's teeth together. Stars exploded before his eyes. Another blow ricocheted off his temple and the world went black for an instant.

When the lights flashed back on he was sitting on

the floor, nestled in a pile of canned goods, staring up blankly.

Sunkiller delivered a kick to his face for good measure that sent him over on to his side.

Calin groaned, forcing himself up on to an elbow and tried to get to his hands and knees.

Sunkiller kicked him again, sending him over on to his back.

Memories flashed before Calin's mind, memories of the beating he'd received fifteen years ago at the hands of Jared Brett. He had failed again, failed to protect Annette Pickler, lost a fight to another man when it counted most.

A laugh came from above him. He tried to focus his blurry gaze on Sunkiller's face.

With the back of his hand, the Ute wiped a snake of blood from his mouth as he peered down at Calin.

'Fifteen years has changed you, white man . . .' Sunkiller muttered, voice hoarse. 'You are not so much the coward now. Perhaps because this woman isn't red, or perhaps because something inside you has changed. It does not matter. You won't be able to stop what's going to happen. And the next time I stand over you this way it will be to cut off your hands.'

Calin tried to push himself up. Sunkiller kicked him back down again.

The Ute peered at him for a dragging moment, then glanced at Annette Pickler, who was standing to the side, hands to her mouth, tears running from her frightened eyes. 'I'll deal with you when I'm through with the others . . .' Sunkiller's voice came low, cold. A dark smile filtered on to his lips.

With a final glance at Calin, the Ute left the store.

Annette Pickler hurried over to Calin, who was halfway up on to his knees, panting, blood dribbling from his mouth and nose. She helped him up, guided him to a chair beside the counter.

She disappeared into the back room, returning a moment later with a basin and a cloth. After setting the basin on the counter, she hovered over him, dabbed the cloth into the water, then blotted the blood from his face.

'You should leave this town, Calin, and never look back,' she said, voice trembling.

'That what you really want?' he asked, getting his breath back, then gritting his teeth as a spike of pain shot through his ribs.

She peered at him, sympathy and something deeper in her eyes. 'No. No, it's not what I want but it's what is best. You said you would protect me from him, but how will you protect yourself? I lost my husband to men of violence. I don't think I could bear losing someone else I might grow to care about . . .'

'If I leave he'll kill Sally Ann Brett and that little girl. He'll kill you.'

She nodded and he stood, legs a little wobbly.

Annette frowned, resignation on her face. 'Maybe that's the way things are meant to be.'

'Only if you let them be.'

She turned away, tears rushing back into her eyes, folded her arms about herself. 'Please, go now, Mr Travers.'

He nodded, located his hat, then walked from the store. Pain radiated from every corner of his body, but a deeper pain burned inside, in a place he'd never known existed, the pain of knowing that maybe Joe Sunkiller could take something from him after all – the chance of a life without loneliness.

Calin wandered back towards the café, hoping Tompkins might still be there. If there was one bright spot in his loss to the Ute it was the fact that Sunkiller had provided him with a means to put him in a jail cell for at least a few days on an assault charge while he figured out which trail to take next.

A shout stopped him and he glanced at the opposite boardwalk to see Tompkins coming out of his office, motioning to him.

'Was just comin' lookin' for you, Hank,' Calin said, after he'd crossed the street and met the marshal.

'Come inside.' A grim look narrowed the lawman's eyes and deepened the lines in his brow.

They went into Tompkins's office, the marshal closing the door behind them.

'Oh, Christ . . .' Calin froze, peering at the bank of cells at the back.

In his cell Jim Foster hung from the bars, a belt wrapped about his throat, his face blue, tongue protruding.

'Hanged himself with his own belt. Never thought he possessed the faculties even to try something like that.' Sorrow laced the marshal's tone. He went to his desk and grabbed the key to the cell. Calin followed him over to the cell and after the marshal unlocked the door, helped get Jim Foster down and on to the cot.

Calin's belly twisted with remorse for a man he'd disliked years back but now could feel only pity for.

'Reckon Sunkiller's responsible for another death, if indirectly.' Calin turned away from the body and wandered back out into the office.

Tompkins followed him out, closed the cell door. 'Well, that does it. Any chance of us having a witness against Sunkiller just died with Jim Foster.'

Calin nodded. ' 'Less we find the child fast. 'Fraid if Sunkiller's got her there ain't much point in keeping her alive with Foster dead.'

Tompkins nodded, then ducked his chin at Calin. 'What happened to you?'

'Sunkiller walked in on me and Annette Pickler . . . *discussing* things. Bring him in, Hank. I'll file charges. Least we can keep him a couple days and buy Brett's wife some time.'

Tompkins nodded. 'Will do.'

'He's dangerous. Best to be cautious.'

'I'd be inclined to just shoot him if he gives me trouble.'

'Couldn't say it wouldn't solve all our problems, least the ones capable of being solved.' He glanced back at the body of Jim Foster, silently promising him if there was a chance at getting his little girl back he would do his best to make it so. He reckoned that was better than a prayer for the man's soul.

CHAPTER NINE

At dawn the next morning Sally Ann Brett stared out through the drawing-room's double windows. Streaks of topaz glazed the grounds and fell across her face and blonde hair. Dark circles nested under her eyes and on her reflection in the glass she could see lines of worry and age creeping in. She held a glass of gin in one hand, and fumbled with the front of her robe with the other. She'd been doing that a lot more lately, she realized, drinking the first thing in the morning. It helped her deal with the days that had somehow become incredibly lonesome and empty, even with all her possessions. Jared made sure, despite his temper, that she lacked for nothing – money, fancy clothes, every convenience that could be shipped here from the East. Everything except companionship, caring, love.

It was her own fault. She'd given up any chance of those things the moment Jared waved all his money under her nose. How could any girl resist that, especially one who had bartered her favors on occasion for a new dress so that for a few hours she could pretend to be one of those fashionable ladies she saw in the magazines that came from back East. When he had offered her the very thing she thought she wanted, she jumped at the chance.

But now she wondered if it was worth the price of what she had given up. When she had thrown herself at the Travers fella, kissed him, she had felt something she had never experienced from Jared: warmth. Jared's kiss was cold, almost brutal, and when he took her, he hurt her. It was not lovemaking, it was simply animal need.

She'd spent most of the night awake, thinking about the things Travers had said about murdered women. Thinking and swallowing glasses of gin. Travers hadn't been lying when he warned Jared they were in danger. But worse than the threat was what she had seen in Jared's eyes when Travers told him.

For despite Jared's coldness, his brutal turns in bed, she had always thought that in some way she was something more than just a possession to him, that somehow, somewhere deep inside he actually did care for her. But his eyes had said different. They said he cared about himself and nothing else. They said she could be replaced as easily as his expensive cigars or Orchard whiskey.

And it had shown her, hard a woman as she had become, that she could still be hurt. That she was still a human being. And that Jared Brett was not.

She had made up her mind to leave; she wasn't

even going to tell him. Jared Brett was a man who did not let go of his possessions. He would never allow her to just walk away from him. So she would wait until he went to town for something, pack a few belongings and a good deal of cash from the safe in the parlor he thought she did not know the combination to, and sneak out. He would never find her where she was going. She would purchase tickets for an east-bound train, disappear from his life and start someplace else with a new name, as a new . . . person.

A sound from behind her interrupted her reverie and she realized the dawn had turned to new morning, the sun now above the trees, splashing the grounds with gold.

She turned, thinking Jared had somehow managed to crawl out of bed early – she expected he wouldn't be up till at least noon after watching him polish off a decanter of whiskey last night to nurse his bruised ego after losing the fight to Travers.

Her breath caught in her throat and the gin glass dropped from her hand. It shattered on the polished floor.

'How did you . . . how did you get in here? Who are you?' Her voice shook, came low, because in her heart she knew who this man was, why he had broken into their home.

The man standing in the middle of the drawing-room grinned. He glanced at the knife in his hand, then back to her. 'You know who I am, Mrs Brett.

I'm sure Calin Travers warned you about me.'

Her lips began to quiver and she knew with everything in her soul that she had made her decision to
leave too late. She might have gotten away with
sneaking out on Jared but she would never escape
this man.

'My husband's—'

'Upstairs, snoring his head off. I climbed up the
trellis. You should lock your windows . . .'

'Get out or I'll scream. He'll come down here.'

The smile he gave her sent chills down her spine.
'Scream if you like. He won't hear you. I hit him
hard enough with my knife handle to make certain
of that. I'll drag his carcass down here after I secure
you.'

His hand drifted beneath his duster, coming back
out with four railroad spikes. He dropped them to
the floor, then came toward her. She tried to back
away, pressing her back against the window. She
wanted to scream but discovered fear locked the
scream in her mind and no sound would come out.
An instant later, her bare foot hit a piece of broken
glass and freed her voice, but before she could get
out a sound the man was on her, his hand jammed
over her mouth, knife pressed against the soft flesh
of her throat.

Calin, sitting on the edge of the bed in his dingy
hotel room, had spent much of the night tossing
and turning, his body paining from the beating
Sunkiller had given him and his mind dwelling on

thoughts of Annette Pickler, Jared Brett, Foster's child and his own past. He'd given much thought to what Tompkins had told him in the café yesterday, and searched his own soul for his responsibility in the events of fifteen years ago. He should have come back to Sundown years ago, but what's done was done and he couldn't change that. But Tompkins was right, he had shown courage trying to stop Brett and the others; he was one against five and nothing he could have done would have stopped them from raping that girl.

He stood, grabbing his gunbelt from the bedpost and strapping it on, gaze absently jumping about the small room done in blue-striped wallpaper, which held little more than a bed, bureau and one hardbacked chair.

No, he had not been a coward and it taken too many years to get it through his thick skull, but he was still responsible for remaining mute afterward and letting those boys get away with what they had done. For that he could only ask for forgiveness. It was time to release the guilt and bring peace and justice to a Ute girl's memory.

He reckoned he would have two or three days at most to figure out a way to find proof against Sunkiller for the killings. That was as long as Tompkins would likely be able to hold him legally. That was all the time he would have to save Sally Ann Brett and somehow persuade Annette Pickler to come forward with any information that might help the case. That was all the time he had to find a missing little girl if she were still alive.

He sighed, resigned to the fact that two days were better than nothing, but still unable to shake a feeling, a dread that it wasn't going to be enough. He grabbed his hat from the chair, set it on his head.

A gentle knock sounded on the door. He paused, hand going to the handle of his Peacemaker.

He went to the door, eased the knob around. As he opened the door, his hand relaxed on the gun. Relief washed over him at the sight of Annette and the little girl at her waist. Annette's hands rested on the girl's shoulders and the girl's eyes were red, rimmed with dark circles. She clung to a ragged doll.

Annette brushed a strand of hair from the girl's face. 'May we come in, Mr Calin?' she asked, and he stepped aside, motioning them into the room. After they were in he closed the door.

'You know who this is?' Annette asked, voice weak, eyes glassy with tears.

He nodded. 'Jim Foster's daughter, I assume.'

Annette nodded. 'She's been out at my place since Joe said he found her wandering. She hasn't said a word in all that time, just cried at night. I heard her sobs. I knew it was wrong, but somehow I convinced myself he was telling me the truth, that he wasn't capable of . . . of the things that happened.' She guided the girl to the bed and the girl sat there, head down. Emotion pulled at Calin's heart. The girl had lost both parents and what lay ahead wasn't going to be easy on her.

He went to the other side of the room, to the window and peered down at the street, waiting for Annette continue. His fingers went white as they gripped the sill and balls of muscle stood out on either side of his jaw. Sunkiller had taken that little girl's parents, heedless of the hell it would cause her, and that made Calin come as close to wanting to kill a man as he had ever come.

Annette came up beside him, touched his shoulder, and he glanced back at her.

'I'm sorry, Calin. I got no excuse for what I did. I was terrified of him, but I really didn't want to believe he was capable of such horrible acts, even after what you said. I kept . . . I kept trying to convince myself you were wrong, that you had made some kind of mistake, but I reckon I knew better.' Tears ran from her eyes. 'I knew he was violent. He beat me sometimes, but . . .' She lowered her voice so the little girl wouldn't hear. 'Killing innocent women in such a way . . .'

'We never want to believe the worst of those close to us, Annette. You did the right thing bringing her here.'

'I never meant to hurt her. I only wanted to protect her. I have a friend in Bannerville. She came during the day to watch the child while I was at the store.'

'Reckon I can't judge you. We all make mistakes, run from things sometimes.'

She looked at the floor, trembling. 'I thought . . . somehow with Jim Foster insane and her mother gone I might . . . provide for her. I know I was foolin' myself.'

'Jim Foster's dead. . .' Calin held his voice to a whisper. 'He hanged himself in the marshal's jail yesterday. That girl's got no one now.'

Tears flowed harder from Annette's eyes. She sobbed and he held her, glancing at the little girl who hung her head and didn't speak.

'Christ, this is a mess,' he said at last. 'In all my years as a manhunter I've never crossed paths with something like this. I don't even have much notion what to do about it.'

'We have to help her, Calin. She deserves it.'

'We will. By now the marshal should have brought Sunkiller in on an assault charge. He's going to hold him a couple days, but if you're willing to testify about that girl we gotta chance of hanging him for those murders.'

She nodded. 'I'll do anything I can to help you. I'll do what's right. But I want you to stay beside me. I need you to be there so I don't falter.'

'You won't falter, Annette. But I'll be there just the same.' He gave her a gentle smile, kissed her forehead. 'I'll go see Tompkins now, tell him what's happened. Stay here with her till I get back.'

She nodded, then went and sat on the bed beside the girl and drew her close.

Calin left them in the room and headed for the marshal's. The marshal was just coming out by the time Calin reached the office.

'You got Sunkiller in a cell?' Calin asked.

Tompkins shook his head. 'Couldn't find hide nor hair of him last night. Made sure a deputy watched the Brett place all night just in case.'

Calin didn't like the notion that the Ute was still free. 'Annette Pickler's in my hotel room. She has Foster's child with her.'

Shock washed over the marshal's face. 'Christ, we got the sonofbitch now, don't we?'

Calin gave him a tentative smile, knowing it wouldn't be over till Sunkiller was sitting in a cell, but hopeful. 'We got him.'

'Let's round up the bastard,' the marshal said. 'I'll take the saloon, you scout out his cabin.'

Calin nodded. He went to livery, saddled his chestnut and a few minutes later approached the front of Joe Sunkiller's cabin. The door hung open and sudden dread crawled through Calin's belly.

He reined up, slid out of the saddle and tethered the reins to a post. He approached the open door cautiously, hand on the grip of his Peacemaker. Easing inside, eyes roving, every sense alert, he scanned the room. The blanket still hung over the back of the chair and the bed appeared as if it hadn't been slept in. Yet on the chair lay the Indian doll trinket.

The dread in Calin's belly strengthened. Something was wrong. His manhunter's sixth sense told him events were moving faster than he had expected. He wagered Tompkins would not find Joe Sunkiller at the saloon, either. Calin had misjudged the Ute, hadn't given him enough credit for cunning. The Ute had guessed Calin would try to bring him in on charges for a day or two and stepped up his plans. That meant there was likely only one other place he'd be.

'Oh, Christ . . .' he mumbled, then spun and ran back outside. He grabbed the reins from the post, mounted, jerked the horse around. His heels slapped the big animal's sides and he drove it into a gallop towards Jared Brett's mansion.

CHAPTER TEN

As Calin reached the perimeter of the mansion, he reined to a halt. He'd spotted something on the ground, just inside the woods, to his right. He jumped from his horse and looped the reins around a branch.

A body lay on the ground, sprawled on its belly, one arm outstretched. Calin knelt, belly plunging, and turned the body over on to its back. A gory slash ran from ear to ear. A deputy's badge glinted in the morning sunlight.

Sickened, Calin straightened, gazing off at the mansion a hundred yards in the distance.

'You sonofabitch . . .' he whispered.

He went toward the mansion, leaving his horse behind. Joe Sunkiller had already been here, and at least one man was dead.

Upon reaching the mansion, he took the porch steps with as little noise as possible and moved towards the front door.

You're too late, a voice inside told him. He hadn't

been able to stop what had happened to that girl fifteen years ago and he wouldn't be able to help Sally Ann Brett now. The thought almost paralyzed him, but another voice rose up, told him if he took Sunkiller down now he could still save Annette and Jim Foster's daughter.

He tried the door, finding it unlocked, and that made him hesitate. Sunkiller expected him and had made things easy. Calin was the last piece in the Ute's plan and he intended to end things today.

Calin eased the door open and slipped the Peacemaker from its holster. He brought the gun up beside his cheek. The foyer was empty but sounds came from the drawing-room, mewing sounds.

His heart started to pound as he edged across the foyer to the drawing-room entryway.

He could not have braced himself for the sight that met his eyes. For one of the few times he could recall, he froze, staring in utter horror, on the verge of blacking out.

What had happened to Sally Ann Brett, whose partially skinned body was staked to the floor, would live in his nightmares for the rest of his life. He averted his gaze, nausea flooding his belly and bile surging into his throat.

Tied to the sofa, a quivering mass of humanity, was Jared Brett. Brett was making the mewing sounds, but it was obvious those sounds weren't for his now deceased wife; they were for himself. In the final tally, Jared Brett was the coward. He cared nothing for an innocent woman's demise, only for his own safety against a force he could no longer bully.

It dawned on Calin as he came from his shock that he saw no sign of Joe Sunkiller, but it dawned a second too late.

Something slammed into the side of his head and he stumbled forward, Peacemaker tumbling from his grip and spinning across the floor.

Reacting on instinct, he'd managed to jerk his head left a little and take some of the force from the blow but it left him momentarily stunned. He stayed on his feet, turned to see Joe Sunkiller, who had been standing pressed against the wall to the side of the entrance, holding a bloody Bowie knife. The Ute had hit Calin with the knife hilt.

Calin steadied himself, pain lancing his skull, but senses intact.

Joe Sunkiller laughed. 'I told you you could not stop it, Travers.'

'Christ . . .' Calin mumbled. 'How could you do something so . . . so brutal to an innocent woman?'

Sunkiller stepped forward, glancing at the body. 'Is it truly any more brutal than what this man did to Crying Dove?' Sunkiller's gaze flicked to Brett, who had tears streaming down his face. 'Even now he worries only for his own pitiful life. It appears I was in error thinking the death of his woman would cause him pain. So now I'll burn his house and take his money. I will leave him in the flames so he dies thinking of what he did fifteen years ago.'

'I won't let you.'

'You will have no choice because you will burn with him. Why do you think I made it so easy for you to enter the house?'

Before his words even finished, Joe Sunkiller reversed the knife in his hand and hurled it at Calin. Calin was half-expecting such a move and went sideways the second the Ute's hand shifted. The knife plucked his hat from his head and nearly took his ear off. It rebounded from the bar and landed on the floor near a chair.

Sunkiller wasted no time surveying his work. He leaped at Calin, without fury and with all his skill. He intended to beat Calin again, only this time he would not walk away and leave the manhunter still alive.

Expecting an immediate attack from Sunkiller, Calin arched left, bringing up a knee in the same move. He connected hard to the Ute's thigh. It did little damage other than to make Sunkiller stagger slightly, pause an instant.

Calin took full advantage of the pause, but his balance wasn't set and his looping blow glanced off the Indian's shoulder.

Sunkiller twisted, arcing a sharp punch that landed flush on Calin's cheek. The blow stung like hell, sent him stumbling diagonally to his right a step.

Instinct, he told himself. He had to let all the skill he acquired over the past ten years take over. He couldn't let himself think, had to act on pure reflex.

152

Look into his eyes, Calin. Look into his eyes and time his blows. If you lose this one Annette and that little girl will die along with you. . . .

His green eyes narrowed and locked with Sunkiller's dark gaze. Sunkiller's teeth came together, muscles balling to either side of his jaw and he shuffled forward. Calin pivoted, snapped a bootheel into the Ute's belly. The move surprised the Indian, sent him back a step.

He recovered more quickly than Calin expected, snapped a powerful punch as he lunged at the manhunter. The fist crashed into Calin's nose with a spray of blood and splintering pain. Calin's legs wavered. Sunkiller grinned, knowing another blow like that would put the manhunter on the floor.

Christ, you can't let him win, Calin. You can't let him go on killing—

Sunkiller hit him again, snapping his head sideways. Blood sprayed from his mouth and pain spiked through his teeth. He nearly went down, staggered backward a handful of steps, arms suddenly loose and legs rubbery. Through the roar of pain he heard Brett making pathetic sounds, begging for his life to be spared. Sunkiller looked at the heavyset man and laughed, obviously enjoying the man's cowardice.

A burst of fury surged through Calin. Memories of that day at the creek, when Brett had beaten the hell out of him and refused any mercy to the Ute girl flashed through his mind. He refused to lose again, refused to let the past repeat itself. Instinct wasn't enough now. Rage had to give him strength, rage and every minute of guilt and powerlessness he had felt for the past fifteen years.

'I ... will ... not ... lose ...' he said through gritted teeth, blood running freely from his mouth and nose.

Sunkiller looked at him. Calin roared, legs steadying with a burst of fury-driven adrenaline. He lunged at the Ute, driving his fists with everything he had left. He didn't stop swinging. Blow after blow landed, many bouncing off Sunkiller's arms and shoulders, but some getting through. The Ute's face took on a look of disbelief at the very fury of Calin's assault. He hadn't expected it, overconfident from his victory at the store. The Ute couldn't set himself to throw back, merely kept his forearms up to defend his face. He was likely banking on Calin tiring himself out.

But he didn't tire. He wouldn't let himself tire. He let out a yell and arced two uppercuts that knifed through the Ute's guard and snapped his head back. He followed immediately with a left hook into the Indian's jaw.

For the first time a blank expression washed across Sunkiller's face. On instinct he tried to fight back but the blows that had landed on his arms and shoulders had brought his guard down and sapped his strength. His punches landed with less strength, were easier to avoid.

Muscles quivering, Calin poured all he had left into each blow. Sunkiller stared to shake.

Calin shook as well, but didn't let up. He could no longer breathe, merely gasp. Sweat streamed down his face and chest. He wouldn't be able to keep it up much longer; only pure willpower drove him now.

He hit Sunkiller full in the mouth. Knuckles collided with teeth with the sound of a gunshot. Sunkiller staggered. Calin hit him again, arcing a blow off the Ute's temple.

Sunkiller's eyes clouded over. Calin planted his trembling legs, setting himself, pistoning a left, then a right. Sunkiller's head snapped back and forth as if it weren't attached.

The Ute froze, blew out a spray of blood. Then he fell face forward, slammed into the floor and didn't move. Blood bubbled from his lips and his breath rasped out.

Calin kicked him full in the face with a heel, making sure the man got no chance to recover, because if he got up Calin knew he wouldn't be able to put him down again.

He stood panting over the fallen Ute, fighting not to collapse himself. He sucked in great gulps of air, shaking all over. His belly threatened to come up.

Turning his head toward Brett, who had gone silent with Calin's win, he peered coldly at the man who years ago had made a decision that had brought so many pain.

'You're going to admit to what you did to that Indian girl fifteen years ago, Brett,' Calin said, barely able to rasp the words out.

Arrogance and defiance came back into Brett's eyes. 'You go to hell, Travers. I ain't admittin' to nothin'.'

'Then I'll see to it Tompkins puts you in a cell with Sunkiller. How long do you think you'd last?'

Brett's eyes narrowed. 'You wouldn't do that, Travers. I know your type.'

'Maybe he wouldn't but I would,' came a voice behind them. Calin swung his head to see Marshal Tompkins standing in the drawing-room entryway, gun drawn. The lawman's face was bleached, his gaze locked on the body of Sally Ann Brett. 'I got no qualms whatsoever over lettin' the Devil sort out who gets his neck stretched.'

The arrogance faded from Brett's eyes and defeat crossed his face. 'You ain't got no right, Tompkins. That girl, she was teasing us. She wanted it.'

Calin's belly tightened. 'I reckon we both just heard a confession, Hank.'

The marshal nodded. 'Good enough for me.'

On the floor Joe Sunkiller suddenly came up and made a grab for his knife, which lay a few feet away. The marshal's gun went off, filling the room with thunder.

Sunkiller jerked, dropped back to the floor, a bullet in his shoulder. He lay there, breathing heavily.

'You ain't getting out that easy, Sunkiller,' said Tompkins. 'You'll hang for what you did.' Tompkins's free hand went to his waist, plucking

156

loose a set of hand-shackles. He tossed them to Calin.

Calin went to Sunkiller, jerked the Ute's hands behind his back and locked the cuffs about his wrists.

The marshal cut Brett loose as Calin retrieved his Peacemaker and kept it aimed at Brett.

'How'd you know where I'd be?' he asked Tompkins, jabbing the barrel into Brett's back to make him walk towards the door.

'Went to Sunkiller's cabin after I didn't find him at the saloon. Since neither of you was there, it was a fair bet where I'd find you. Wish I had got here sooner.' He cast a final glance at Sally Ann Brett and shuddered, then went to Sunkiller and forced him to his feet.

'Fifteen years sooner . . .' Calin said.

EPILOGUE

Three days later, Calin Travers walked toward the general store. Both Jared Brett and Joe Sunkiller were in a cell, Brett having signed a confession to his role in the Indian girl's rape. Calin wondered whether Tompkins wasn't still of a mind to throw the sonofabitch in with Sunkiller and save the town the cost of feeding him.

Beside Calin, her small hand in his, walked Clarissa Foster, who now had no parents and the prospect of years suffering with the loss and the trauma she'd been through. She still held her ragged doll. He and the marshal had talked over sending her to a home, but Calin reckoned maybe a better option existed, one that might give the little girl a chance at a half-normal life.

He reached the general store and entered. Annette Pickler looked over at them as they came in, then ran towards them. She grabbed the little girl, hugged her close. The girl barely responded, but maybe with time things would be different.

'Marshal and I are of a like mind, Annette. Foundling home would do this little girl no good. She's lost enough. We figure with you she's got chance. That is, if you're willing . . .'

Annette stood, tears shimmering in her eyes. 'I'll take care of her as if she was my own, Calin. You know that.'

He smiled. 'Reckon I do.'

'But the marshal . . . he doesn't want to press charges against me?'

Calin shook his head. 'I asked him not to. He was inclined that way anyway. We both figure you're a good woman or you wouldn't have brought that girl in and agreed to testify against Sunkiller. Sittin' in a jail wouldn't do you or this little girl any good.'

Annette peered into his eyes, searching them, a tear slipping down her cheek. 'Will . . . will you leave . . . now that you got Sunkiller?'

He pulled her face close, gave her a kiss on the cheek. 'Reckon there's more for me in Sundown than I mighta thought.'

'You'll stay? With me?'

He nodded, winked. 'A fella could do worse, I'm bettin'.' He turned to leave, hand on the doorhandle. 'Reckon I ain't half the coward I figured myself to be . . .'